The Red Slippers

Nancy Drew

DIARIES™

The Red Slippers

#11

CAROLYN KEENE

Aladdin

NEW YORK LONDON TORONTO SYDNEY NEW DELHI

ALADDIN
An imprint of Simon & Schuster Children's Publishing Division
1230 Avenue of the Americas, New York, NY 10020
First Aladdin paperback edition December 2015
Text copyright © 2015 by Simon & Schuster, Inc.
Cover illustration copyright © 2015 by Erin McGuire
Also available in an Aladdin hardcover edition.
All rights reserved, including the right of reproduction in whole or in part in any form.
ALADDIN is a trademark of Simon & Schuster, Inc., and related logo
is a registered trademark of Simon & Schuster, Inc.
NANCY DREW, NANCY DREW DIARIES, and related logo are
trademarks of Simon & Schuster, Inc.
For information about special discounts for bulk purchases, please contact
Simon & Schuster Special Sales at 1-866-506-1949 or business@simonandschuster.com.
The Simon & Schuster Speakers Bureau can bring authors to your live event.
For more information or to book an event contact the Simon & Schuster Speakers Bureau
at 1-866-248-3049 or visit our website at www.simonspeakers.com.
Cover designed by Karin Paprocki
Interior designed by Mike Rosamilia
The text of this book was set in Adobe Caslon Pro.
Manufactured in the United States of America 0318 OFF
6 8 10 9 7 5
Library of Congress Control Number 2015951007
ISBN 978-1-4814-3814-8 (hc)
ISBN 978-1-4814-3813-1 (pbk)
ISBN 978-1-4814-3815-5 (eBook)

Contents

Dear Diary,

I ALWAYS FIND IT FUNNY HOW A CASE can come out of nowhere. Like the other day, one minute I'm drinking hot chocolate, the next I find out someone's anonymously harassing an old friend of mine. Maggie Richards is dancing a lead role in the ballet of *Sleeping Beauty*, and someone is threatening to ruin her future career, so I'm on the job. I thought it was going to be an easy case—almost a warm-up for the new year—but boy, was I wrong!

CHAPTER ONE

❧

An Old Friend Returns

"I NEED A THING," BESS SAID WITH A SIGH between sips of hot chocolate.

"Christmas was just last month. What more could you possibly need?" George shot back.

Bess rolled her eyes. "Not like that. I mean a thing that defines who I am."

"I don't get it. We all know who you are. You're Bess," George said with a shrug, turning her attention back to a game on her phone.

George and Bess are cousins and my two best friends. Even though they seem like total opposites—George doesn't care about looks or clothes, while Bess is a bit of a fashionista; George loves technology and always has the latest gadget, while Bess prefers snail mail to e-mail—they're as close as sisters. Sometimes, though, George can get so caught up in her Twitter feed that she doesn't notice the people sitting right in front of her.

In general, I'm somewhere in between: I like to look nice and put together, but I don't keep with the latest trends; and I like my smartphone, but I'm not obsessed with it. Sometimes I have to be a bridge between them. I could tell this was one of those times.

Bess had been acting weird all day. We'd gone into town to do some errands—mostly just to get out of the house—and she had barely said a word. At first I thought it was the weather—a cold snap had moved in overnight with the threat of snow later—but even after we'd stopped at the Coffee Corner, our favorite café in River Heights and George's place of employment, to get warm, she still hadn't cheered up.

"What's going on, Bess?" I asked as gently as I could. Ironically, Bess is the most emotionally intuitive of the three of us. Whenever George or I are upset, Bess knows exactly what to do or say to make us feel better. I wished Bess could talk to Bess, but I'd try my best instead.

"Remember New Year's Eve?" Bess asked.

I nodded. Bess's parents throw a big party every New Year's Eve. Each year they pick a different theme. One year it was An Evening in Wonderland, and they hung at least a hundred different clocks on the walls, replaced the furniture in one room with doll furniture, spread stuffed bunnies throughout the house, and made place mats out of playing cards. They even hung half a mannequin dressed in a light-blue dress with a white apron from the hallway ceiling, so it looked like Alice was falling through the rabbit hole into the house. It was always the party of the year, and half of River Heights attended.

George, Bess, and I have been going to that party for as long as we can remember. When we were younger,

Bess's parents would herd us up to her room and we'd be asleep long before midnight. As we got older, we kept the tradition of heading up to Bess's room early, only now we watched the ball drop in Times Square on TV, drank glasses of sparkling cider, and shared our resolutions for the coming year.

This year had been no different. The theme of the party had been the 1960s, and George, Bess, and Ned, my boyfriend, had scoured As You Wore, the vintage shop in town, for the perfect outfits. Bess's parents had outdone themselves with the decorations. Entering the house felt like stepping through a time warp. The walls, the furniture, and the rugs were all from the 1960s or earlier. They'd even swapped out their TV for an older model. We ate a ton of food, danced, took goofy pictures in the photo booth the Marvins had rented, and headed up to Bess's room to watch the ball drop. It had seemed like Bess was having as good a time as the rest of us, so I couldn't imagine what would have made her upset.

"Sure. I remember New Year's," I said.

"Do you remember my resolution?" Bess asked.

I thought back, but it wasn't coming to mind. Bess noticed my hesitancy. "George said she wanted to crack five thousand followers on Twitter. Ned said he wanted to make the dean's list. You said you wanted to beat your personal record for solving a case."

Suddenly it all came rushing back. "You said you wanted to floss more," I said.

Bess nodded glumly. I could see tears brimming in her eyes, and I felt like a horrible friend because I still didn't know why this was making her so upset.

It was especially frustrating because I'm an amateur detective. I help people track down stolen goods, or figure out who's behind a blackmail attempt. My dad's a prosecutor, and he says that I solve more cases than some of the detectives he works with, so I should have been able to put the clues together and figure out why Bess was so sad. I understood that flossing wasn't the most exciting resolution in the world, but it didn't seem worth crying over.

Fortunately, Bess noticed my confusion. "You all have your things. Like George is a computer nerd."

"Hey!" George piped up. She had finally noticed Bess's mood and had put down her phone.

"Excuse me. A computer *geek*," Bess corrected.

"Thank you," George replied.

"You're a detective. Ned is a brain. But I don't know who I am or what I'm good at or even what I want to be when I get older."

I thought for a second before answering, because I wanted to get this right. I finally understood what Bess was saying, and there was some truth to it: she wasn't as easily categorized as me, George, or even Ned, but that didn't mean she had no identity.

"You're the most compassionate and empathetic person I've ever met, Bess," I said finally.

"That's different," Bess countered.

"Yes, but it's still an amazing ability. Don't dismiss that."

"She's right," George agreed. "People *like* you; that's a skill! Besides, lots of people our age don't know what they're good at or what they're going to be when they grow up. You have time to figure it out."

Before we could try to console Bess any further, the café's door flew open and a voice boomed out, "Nancy Drew and Bess Marvin? I thought I saw you through the window!"

Bess and I turned. A tall, statuesque girl stood in the doorway, looking at us expectantly.

Bess and I exchanged a confused glance. Neither of us had any idea who she was.

The girl didn't seem to realize our obliviousness and approached our table with a big grin on her face. "I'm going to grab some green tea, but then we have so much to catch up on!"

I sat there with a frozen smile on my face, not sure how to respond. "We can't wait to find out about you as well," Bess said genuinely. That's what I mean about Bess being a people person. She always knows exactly what to say and never makes anyone feel uncomfortable.

The girl smiled broadly. "I'll be back in a minute," she said, and got in line to buy her tea.

"Who is that?" George asked once she was out of hearing range.

"I have no idea," I answered.

"Me neither," Bess confirmed.

"Well, this is going to be supremely awkward if you don't figure out who she is before she gets back," George said.

The girl was just waiting for the barista to pour her hot water. She waved at us with a smile. Bess and I smiled back.

Bess turned toward me urgently. "You need to solve this case and figure out who she is."

By my estimate the girl would be back at our table in less than a minute. There wasn't time to do much investigating.

I studied her as discreetly as I could, looking for any important details. Her hair hung loose, just brushing her shoulders, but instead of parting in the middle, it flowed back, as if she wore her hair tied back most of the time. She was carrying a small duffel bag; it looked like a gym bag but had a pink satin ribbon poking out of it. I knew that was important, but I couldn't figure out what it signified. She wore a skirt, and I noticed the muscular definition of her calves through her tights. She was absentmindedly rotating her ankle, turning her foot out at a ninety-degree angle.

All of a sudden, a memory flooded back—standing behind a girl doing the same move in Miss Taylor's ballet class eight years ago.

As the girl approached us, I could feel Bess's nervous eyes on me. I stood up, holding my arms out for a hug. "Maggie," I said. "It's so good to see you again!"

"George," I said, "this is Maggie Richards. She was in Miss Taylor's ballet class with Bess and me."

"But then she moved to Cleveland to attend a prestigious ballet academy," Bess continued, her face alight in recognition.

Maggie nodded, blushing a little.

"From our very first class," I explained, "it was clear Maggie was a star."

"Oh, that's not true," Maggie said bashfully.

But it *was* true. Even at five years old, you could tell that Maggie truly had a gift. Miss Taylor was always complimenting Maggie on her technique, her extension, and her line, but more than that, there was something inherently expressive about the way she moved. When she danced the part of one of the polichinelles (the children who emerge from Mother Ginger's skirt) in *The Nutcracker*, you could see true joy in her movements. Even just doing barre work, the exercises we did to warm up, you couldn't take your eyes off Maggie. She was magnetic. No one had been surprised when she was accepted into the Cleveland Ballet Academy to train as a professional ballerina.

"What are you doing back in town?" Bess asked.

"I'm in a touring production of *Sleeping Beauty*, and there's a performance tomorrow in River Heights," Maggie explained.

"That's great!" I exclaimed. "Does this mean you're a prima ballerina now?"

Maggie shook her head. "Not yet, but this tour is specifically for the most promising dancers in the region. They auditioned dancers from the top dance schools in three states. It's to give us a taste of what touring would feel like if we did turn professional."

"Fantastic," Bess said. "We're so happy for you!"

Maggie looked around the shop for a second, then leaned in close, as if she was going to tell us a secret. "Actually, this River Heights performance could be my big break," she whispered.

"How so?" I asked.

"Supposedly, Oscar LeVigne will be in attendance."

For the second time that day, Bess and I exchanged confused glances. We didn't have any idea who Oscar LeVigne was.

Maggie noticed and started laughing. "Wow, you guys must have quit ballet ages ago if you've forgotten Oscar LeVigne. Miss Taylor used to talk about him all the time."

I shrugged. "Yeah, I stopped in middle school. I just didn't have the time with my cases."

"Cases?" Maggie asked. "Like a detective?"

I nodded as she tried to process this. People always seem surprised when they find out I'm an amateur sleuth.

"I do remember you always reading mysteries before

class," Maggie remembered. "What about you, Bess? You were a really talented dancer, if I recall."

Bess blushed. "I just lost my passion for it. I felt like I wasn't getting any better and I'd never be as good as I wanted to be." She paused for a moment. "I do miss it sometimes."

"Well," Maggie continued, "Oscar LeVigne is a famous ballet critic. He's known for spotting upcoming stars. A review from him can make or break careers. If I get a good one, there's a really good chance I'll be asked to audition for a professional company. If I get a bad one . . . I don't even want to *think* about it."

"I'm sure you'll do great," I said.

"Yeah, and we'll be there cheering you on," Bess said. "Just like we were at the recital when the ballet academy scout showed up all those years ago."

Maggie gave us a grateful smile. "It's so good to see you two. I've missed you."

"You too," Bess said.

"I'd love to stay and chat, but I have to get to rehearsal by three o'clock and I can't be late. Jamison, our choreographer and my teacher at the academy, is really strict. You have to do an extra *grand plié* for every minute you're late; if you're more than twenty minutes late, you sit out the next performance. Maybe we could meet for dinner later?"

"That sounds great," I said.

"Wait," George interrupted. "Did you say three o'clock?"

Maggie nodded.

"But it's ten after three right now!" George exclaimed, holding out her watch.

"What!?" Maggie practically shrieked. "My phone says it's ten after two!"

❧

CHAPTER TWO

Frenemies

GEORGE HELD OUT HER WRIST. "THIS IS A satellite watch. It's accurate to the nanosecond," she said apologetically.

"No, no, no. This cannot be happening. This cannot be happening," Maggie repeated as if in a daze.

"Come on," I said, jumping up. "My car's right out front. Where's the rehearsal?"

"At the River Heights Performing Arts Theater," Maggie replied breathlessly.

"Okay, if we hurry, I can get you there in ten

minutes. You'll be punished, but you won't have to sit out the next performance."

"Thank you so much!" Maggie said, springing up and shrugging on her coat. Bess, George, and I followed suit.

"It's going to be tight," Bess whispered into my ear as we raced toward the car. She was right. We would need to get really lucky to make it there in less than ten minutes, but it was worth a shot.

We piled into my car, George riding shotgun with Bess and Maggie in the back.

I started the engine and pulled into traffic.

"Take a left on Maple," George said.

"Are you sure?" I asked George. "The most direct route is down Elm."

George nodded, staring at the GPS on her phone. "There's construction about a mile down Elm. It goes down to one lane. Maple's faster."

I nodded and checked my blind spot before slipping into the left lane.

Maggie was still in a daze. "I just don't understand how this happened," she murmured.

I didn't either. I had never heard of a cell phone being off by an hour. I thought they were all connected to one tower. Maybe they weren't as accurate as George's satellite watch, but they shouldn't be that wrong.

"Bess," I said, as I hung a left onto Maple, pushing down a little harder on the gas. "Take over navigating for George. Maggie, give George your phone so she can figure out how this happened."

They exchanged phones, and out of the corner of my eye I could see George's fingers tapping and swiping the screen, moving so fast they were almost a blur. A bomb could have gone off and she wouldn't have noticed.

"Right on Oak," Bess shouted from the back. Oak was in just a few feet. I hit the brakes and took the corner faster than I should have.

I checked the rearview mirror and could see Maggie chewing on her lip, doing her best to hold back tears. She let out a muffled wail. "We only have four minutes! We're never going to make it."

I pushed down a little harder on the gas. "We're cutting it close, but it's not hopeless," I told her. I was now going four miles over the speed limit. I knew Maggie wanted me to go faster, but if I got pulled over—or worse, got in an accident—that would just make us even later.

"There!" George suddenly exclaimed, thrusting the phone behind her to show Maggie and Bess.

"What are you showing us?" Bess asked.

"See that app there? TikTok?"

In the rearview mirror, I could see Bess and Maggie peering forward. "I see it!" Bess said. "Nancy, left on Spruce."

"Got it," I said, maneuvering into the left lane. "How does the app work?" I asked George.

"It allows people to manually set the time. It's designed for people who are chronically late. They can set their phone to be five, ten, fifteen minutes ahead, whatever they want, to trick themselves into being on time."

"Did you install that app?" Bess asked.

Maggie shook her head. "No, definitely not!"

"Maybe someone deliberately put it on your phone to make you late!" Bess suggested.

"Did you let anyone use your phone today?" I asked, as I checked my blind spot and swerved into the next lane to get around the slowpoke driver in front of me. I knew from my time in Miss Taylor's class that ballet was extremely competitive and people would do anything to get ahead, but something like this seemed completely out of line. I didn't understand who would want to get ahead by hurting people.

"Nancy's in detective mode already!" George said. "She'll figure out who sabotaged you in no time."

"Thanks, Nancy," Maggie said, "but this is no mystery. I know exactly who did it."

"Who?" Bess asked.

"Fiona Scott," Maggie replied, practically spitting the name. "She's my understudy. If Jamison doesn't let me perform tomorrow for Oscar LeVigne, Fiona will go on instead."

"That reminds of me this old movie I watched with my grandmother, *All About Eve*. It's about an understudy who schemes to take over for the star without anyone knowing," George said.

"Unfortunately, this isn't a movie," Maggie lamented.

"How do you know it's Fiona?" I asked. I had learned over the years that the first person someone suspects is usually the wrong one.

"This isn't the first incident that's happened on this tour. In Fairview, my wig went missing thirty minutes before the start of the performance. Fiona had to step in, since her wig is two sizes smaller than mine and there wasn't an extra. Then in Bristol someone told our hotel's front desk to give me a wake-up call every two hours the night before our show. The next day I was so tired, I fainted backstage during intermission and Fiona had to take over in the second act."

"How has this girl not been kicked out of the company?" Bess fumed. Her face was red with indignation. Bess hates anything that isn't fair, and cheating drives her especially crazy.

"There was never any proof," Maggie said. "Plus Fiona's parents are major academy donors. Their money helps pay for Jamison's salary. He is never going to punish her without evidence and risk losing her parents as benefactors."

"I'm sure Nancy could end this once and for all," Bess said.

"I'd be happy to look into it," I offered.

"It's okay," Maggie said. "This is our second-to-last stop on the tour. I'd rather just focus on dancing and stay out of Fiona's way. I don't want to make her any angrier."

I caught Bess's eye in the rearview mirror. Next to me, George was looking at me the same way. None of us thought Maggie's plan was a good one. From what she had said so far, Fiona seemed ruthless. Maggie couldn't be careful enough!

But before I could say anything further, we were at the theater. I screeched to a stop.

"It's too late!" Maggie said. "Three twenty."

"You have twenty-eight seconds till it turns three twenty-one," George said, holding up her watch. "I'll run in right behind you to prove you made it in time."

"We all will," I said.

We jumped out of the car and Maggie sprinted up the steps, with George, Bess, and me right behind her.

Maggie flung open the door and raced through the lobby.

"Fifteen seconds!" George shouted breathlessly.

Maggie made it to the theater entrance and threw open the door, stopping so abruptly that I almost plowed into her. I looked up and saw why she had stopped so suddenly.

The entire cast—roughly thirty-five girls and a handful of boys—stood staring at Maggie, in complete silence. There was a mix of horrified looks on their faces as well as the occasional gleeful one. The back of Maggie's neck was bright red, and I imagined that her face was as well. This wasn't a room you wanted to walk into late.

Only one person wasn't looking at Maggie. Standing with his back to us was a man with blond hair. The cast members kept shifting their eyes from Maggie to him and back. I had a feeling it wasn't going to be pleasant when he finally did turn around.

After what seemed like several minutes of awkward silence, George cleared her throat. "I have the most accurate watch money can buy. . . . Maggie made it here with five seconds to spare. She should get to dance tomorrow."

Slowly the man turned. In front of me, Maggie caught her breath. Bess squeezed my hand.

"I'm sorry," Maggie squeaked.

"You're sorry?" the man asked in an eerily calm voice. His entire body was held so rigidly, I didn't understand how he'd managed to turn around so smoothly. It looked like he was rotating on a lazy Susan. His hair was slicked back and he had piercing blue eyes with extremely well-defined cheekbones. He was handsome, but severe. He also didn't seem like someone you wanted to be on the bad side of, which, unfortunately, was exactly where Maggie was standing.

"You're sorry?" he repeated, a smidgen louder than before.

Maggie nodded.

"YOU'RE SORRY!?" he bellowed this time with amazing force. If we were in a cartoon, we'd be leaning back from the power of his voice.

Maggie nodded again. The man marched toward us. "I thought you were serious, Maggie. I thought you had the ability to go far. Was I wrong about you?"

"No . . . ," Maggie said meekly.

"I don't care if you were technically under twenty-one minutes late, as this"—he paused and gave George a dismissive once-over—"disheveled little girl claims. If you were serious, you would have been here twenty minutes early, warming up, making sure you were in tip-top shape. Fiona was. Maybe I should let her go on instead of you, anyway." I looked up on the stage and saw a tall blond girl struggling to hide an ear-to-ear grin.

"That must be Fiona," I whispered to Bess and George.

"Please," Maggie said to Jamison. "The time on my phone—"

Jamison cut her off. "Stop!" he roared. "How do I feel about excuses?"

"You hate them."

Jamison grabbed Maggie by the back of the neck and marched her toward the stage. He didn't seem to be hurting her, but it certainly seemed humiliating. "I just don't understand how you could do this to me. I thought we were a team; I thought we were going to impress Oscar together. You've let me down. You'll have to dance the best you've ever danced today to prove to me that you can do this. If not, Fiona's up."

Once Maggie was onstage, everyone sprang into action. Fiona couldn't hide her look of disappointment, but she got out of the way and let Maggie take her spot.

"Let's take it from the top," Jamison said. "Everyone back to starting positions."

I sighed a deep breath of relief and slumped into a nearby seat. The adrenaline rush from the drive was starting to wear off, and I was exhausted. Bess and George sat next to me.

"That was intense!" George said.

Bess nodded in agreement. "At least he's giving

Maggie a shot. Your race-car driving wasn't all for naught, Nancy."

George giggled. "Who knew you could maneuver a car like that! You were like a female Jeff Gordon out there."

"I was never unsafe," I protested. "Just a little more aggressive than usual."

"I'm not complaining," George said. "I wish you drove like that all the time."

I grinned but shook my head. I preferred a calmer style of driving. I watched the stage, where Jamison was pacing and speaking to Maggie. He seemed upset, but I couldn't hear what he was saying.

"You know what's weird?" I asked my friends.

"What?" Bess said.

"Jamison seemed just as upset as Maggie was. It seemed like he took it really personally," I noted.

"That's because Jamison has as much riding on Oscar LeVigne's review as Maggie does," a male voice said. We all swiveled our heads to see a thin boy about our age with messy dark hair sitting a few seats down, almost entirely hidden in the darkness. "I'm Sebastian," the boy said, sliding over to sit closer to us.

"Nice to meet you," I said. "I'm Nancy and this is Bess and George. Do you have a friend in the production as well?"

He shook his head. "I'm the pianist accompanying the show." I noticed his long and thin hands; they looked like they were made to play the piano.

"What do you mean about Jamison having as much riding on this performance as Maggie?" I asked.

Sebastian shrugged. "Just like it was really competitive for the dancers to get selected for this tour, all the top teachers in the area wanted the job choreographing it. Jamison is known as a teacher who gets results, but what he really wants to do is choreograph. If Oscar likes what he did, it will open a lot of doors for Jamison. If he doesn't, it will be tough for him to get another opportunity to break through."

I nodded. "But why does that make him so mad at Maggie? Can't Fiona dance the part just as well?"

Sebastian grunted dismissively. "She wishes. The

Lilac Fairy, as Jamison choreographed it, is a hugely technical role. To dance that part and make it look effortless takes great skill. Maggie's the only person in the company who can do it justice. When Fiona dances it, you can see the gears turning in her head as she remembers each step. It's very mechanical. Fiona tries hard and her parents have given her every opportunity, but she's just not at the right level."

"Sebastian!" Jamison bellowed from the front of the room. "Stop flirting and get down here, please!"

I blushed, but Sebastian seemed unfazed. "That's my cue. See you later." He strode to the front of the room and took his seat at the piano.

I looked at my friends. "Do you guys want to head home?" I asked. They nodded. As we made our way into the lobby, we bumped into our old ballet teacher, Miss Taylor.

"Nancy, Bess! It's so nice to see you!" she said. "I still miss you in my class, Bess. You too, Nancy."

It was no secret that Bess was the more talented dancer of the two of us. I thought back to how

Sebastian had described Fiona. That was probably a fair description of how I danced. I tried hard, but it never felt natural. I never became lost in the music the way Bess did. I was always thinking about the next step, concentrating on how I held my shoulders or my hip rotation.

"Are you involved in this show?" Bess asked.

A cloud briefly passed over Miss Taylor's face before she regained her composure. "No, I'm just helping out. Tomorrow my advanced students get to observe the preperformance rehearsal and even warm up with the company."

"That sounds like a wonderful opportunity," Bess said.

Miss Taylor gave us a tight grin. "It's a great honor . . . for them." There was an awkward pause as we tried to think of something to say. "Do you girls mind doing me a favor?" Miss Taylor asked. "Can you put these posters for the performance around town?"

I looked at Bess and George. We didn't have any other plans. "Sure," we said in unison.

I took the roll of posters from Miss Taylor, and we headed back out into the cold. Before I had even finished opening the door, I heard a man's voice shouting.

"It's bad enough that you and your mother convinced me to let you go to dance school! But going behind my back to tour with a company? Having the family name on a ballet poster all over town? It's the last straw!"

Tentatively I pushed open the door and saw a man yelling at what I guessed was his son. The boy was shivering in his ballet clothes, looking furious. We held back, not wanting to make the situation worse.

"Get in the car, Colin," the man yelled. "We're going home."

"No!" Colin yelled back. "I have a rehearsal." He stormed back to the theater, shouting, "I'm becoming a professional dancer. Get used to seeing my name everywhere!" He pushed past us, letting out a primal scream of rage as he went.

"We'll see about that!" his dad screamed back. He

ran to the door and tried to open it, but it was locked.

"I hate you!" Colin yelled from inside.

His dad kicked the ground in anger before turning and heading to his car.

"What's up?" I asked George, noting that she looked particularly glum.

"It's nothing. That fight just reminded me of the fight I had with my mom when I told her I didn't want to join ballet with you and Bess. I wanted to join the robotics club. She was upset that I didn't want to do the same things that most girls want to do."

Bess rubbed George's back. "I know it's upsetting, and I'm not saying your mom or Colin's dad handled the situation well, but their intentions were good. They just wanted to prevent their kids from being teased."

George shrugged. "I think a parent's job is to let their kids be who they are and to support them no matter what."

I stopped at a light pole in front of my car, thinking this would be a good place to hang a poster. But when I unrolled one, I froze.

"Guys," I said. "We have a bigger problem."

"What's going on?" Bess asked.

I held up the poster. Although it listed all the dancers' names, including a special citation for Colin Carter as the Prince, the picture was of Maggie in an arabesque—a ballet position where you stand on one leg, your other leg in the air behind you, and your arms extended, one in front and one in back.

Only the picture had been vandalized—and Maggie's face was violently scratched out.

CHAPTER THREE

~❧~

On the Case

"OH MY GOSH!" BESS EXCLAIMED. "ARE THEY all like that?"

I flipped through the rest. Every single one had been defaced, but the posters themselves didn't seem to have been tampered with. Clearly someone had altered the file that had gone to the printer.

"Who would do something like this?" Bess asked.

"I can think of one person, at least," George said drolly.

I nodded. "It does seem pretty clear that Fiona

has it in for Maggie. Did you see how she smiled as Jamison was yelling at Maggie?"

"Yeah, and I noticed the daggers she gave me when I proved that Maggie made it just in the nick of time," George added.

For a moment we were all silent. I was pretty sure we were all thinking the same thing.

George spoke up first. "I know Maggie said she didn't want you to investigate Fiona, but whoever did this," she said, gesturing to the poster, "seems really scary."

George was right. The black lines completely obliterating Maggie's face showed that the culprit must have been really angry. I know ballet is cutthroat, but this seemed personal, like it was about hurting Maggie.

"I agree," I said. "We have to convince her to let us investigate."

I turned toward the theater, but before I had taken two steps, Bess's voice stopped me. "Wait. Are you sure this is a good idea?"

I turned back, my forehead wrinkled in confusion. I may be the official detective in the group, but my friends are always right by my side. They've never shied away from a case, especially when we think someone might be in danger. I couldn't imagine why Bess might not want me to investigate further.

"Fiona needs to be stopped," I said. "You heard what Maggie said in the car: without hard proof, nothing will happen to her."

"Of course Fiona needs to be stopped," Bess said. "I'm just wondering if we need to tell Maggie. Do you remember our ballet recitals growing up?"

"Of course," I replied. Miss Taylor's classes put on two recitals a year: one in June and one in December. It didn't matter that the recitals were small and the audiences consisted of friends and family; everyone took them as seriously as if we were dancing at Lincoln Center in New York. The weeks leading up the performance, I would practice morning, noon, and night. My dad had to make a rule banning jetés before seven a.m. because my leaps woke him up.

"Do you remember what happened to Maggie before every recital?" Bess asked, breaking into my reverie.

I thought for a second, and it all came rushing back: Maggie sitting in the corner, wide-eyed, trembling with nerves, pale as a ghost. "Stage fright. We were all nervous, but she was on a whole different level."

Bess nodded. "It didn't matter that she was the best by far. She was so anxious, she threw up before every performance. Imagine how nervous she is about dancing for Oscar. Maybe we shouldn't show her the posters."

Bess had a valid point. I was doing this to help Maggie. It wouldn't do any good to make her more stressed before the performance. What if she made a mistake in front of Oscar because of the poster? On the other hand, it seemed wrong to investigate Fiona without Maggie's permission, especially since she had explicitly asked me not to.

As I examined the poster again, the solution suddenly occurred to me.

"We're not going to investigate Fiona," I announced. Bess and George looked at me in shock.

George leaned forward and placed her hand on my forehead. "Are you feeling all right, Nancy?"

I grinned. "I didn't say I'm not taking on the case. I just said we're not going to investigate *Fiona*."

"I don't get it," George said.

"We're going to investigate the poster. We're going to find out who vandalized the file. But we'll ignore the other acts of sabotage and pretend Maggie never said anything to us about Fiona. When we know who vandalized the poster, we can tell Maggie, and then she can decide what to do."

Bess and George smiled.

"All right, what's the first step, boss?" George asked.

I looked at the tube the posters had come in and noted a sticker that read SHARP IMAGE. "Bess, you stay here and keep an eye on Maggie. We might not officially be investigating Fiona, but I don't trust her. Don't let Maggie be alone, and if anything suspicious happens, call me right away."

Bess nodded.

"George," I continued, "you and I are going to Sharp Image to see what we can find out about whoever submitted this file for printing."

"Sounds good, Nancy," Bess said as she headed back into the theater.

Sharp Image is a regional chain. They're known for their sterile white walls and counters, with giant photos of animals and landscapes adorning the walls, showcasing the bright and clean printing jobs. What most people know them for, though, are the hot-pink vests and hats they require all employees to wear. It is widely regarded as one of the most humiliating uniforms in River Heights, and most of the employees look positively miserable in them.

I knew that what I was going to ask was technically against the store's policies, but I was hoping the clerk would be annoyed enough by the job that he or she wouldn't mind helping me.

George and I walked in and saw a young man

behind the counter with his back to the door. He had earbuds in, which explained why he didn't hear the bell that had announced our presence.

I plastered a big smile onto my face, prepared to be charming. As he turned, however, my stomach sank. This wasn't going to be nearly as easy as I had hoped.

"Derek Chase . . . ," I said, unable to keep the dismay out of my voice.

"Nancy Drew," he answered, sounding as unhappy to see me as I was to see him. "What are you doing here? Ruining someone else's life?"

"I didn't ruin your life, Derek," I answered.

"I beg to differ," he sneered. "I should be raking in millions as an investment banker right now. Instead I'm wearing pink and making minimum wage."

"I didn't force you to cheat," I pointed out to him. "I just caught you."

A friend of my dad's was a business professor at River Heights University. He had a hunch that a student had broken into his office and printed a copy of the final exam. He hadn't wanted to get the officials involved, but he had mentioned it to my dad, who mentioned it to me. I took on the case and ended up busting Derek, who was then kicked out of school. I guess his dreams of working on Wall Street had gone up in smoke too.

A lot of times when I catch a culprit I feel almost as bad for them as I do for the victim. In my experience, people do bad things for good reasons, and many times they break the rules because they feel like they have no other option.

Derek, however, was an exception. He didn't steal the test because he was working three jobs to pay tuition and had no time to study. He stole it because he wanted an easy A. When I'd confronted him, he'd sneered that he couldn't believe a girl had caught him.

"We're helping out a ballet company that's in town. But as we began hanging the posters, we realized there was something wrong with them." I figured it was better not to tell Derek that I was working a case.

"We print what you give us. If there's a problem with the file, that's on you. It's right in the job order's terms and conditions," he said, raising his eyebrow cockily.

"Can I just see the file?" I asked. "So I know what was sent?"

"We can only show the file to the person who sent it," Derek replied. "And I know for a fact that that wasn't you, Nancy Drew, or you, Georgia Fayne," he said, calling George by her full name.

George glowered at him. She hates being called Georgia.

"That's also expressly written in our terms and conditions," he continued smugly, crossing his arms with a satisfied smile. He seemed to be enjoying this.

"Well, how about this?" George said, apparently as frustrated with Derek as I was. "We'd like to pay for some Internet time."

I gave George an approving nod. I knew she was thinking that she could use the network to access the company's main system and get the file that way.

Unfortunately, Derek wasn't dumb—just lazy. He knew exactly what George was thinking. "Sorry, girls.

There will be no hacking of our system today. Our terms and conditions also say we can deny service to anyone, and I'm denying service to you both. Bye-bye now!" He popped his earbuds back in and turned away.

"What do we do now?" George asked.

I was asking myself the same question. This was our only lead so far, and I wasn't sure of our next move.

"I can't believe Derek Chase of all people is derailing our investigation," I muttered.

"Hey, Nancy, look," George said, gesturing toward the wall. I turned to see where she was pointing, and my jaw dropped. Hanging there was a photo of the CEO of the entire Sharp Image chain.

"That's the guy—" George began.

"We saw yelling at his son outside the theater," I finished.

~

CHAPTER FOUR

The Cat in the Chimney Trick

GEORGE OPENED HER MOUTH TO SAY MORE, but I quickly put my finger to my lips. I nodded my head toward Derek as I hustled George out the door. We needed to discuss this new development, but I wanted to talk as far away from his vindictive ears as possible. If he knew I suspected his boss (Michael Carter, according to the photo on the wall), he would come up with a way to sabotage my case in no time.

"I bet you Michael Carter destroyed the posters

because he was mad about Colin dancing," George burst out as soon as the door closed behind us.

"He did seem incredibly angry," I acknowledged.

"More than angry," George countered. "He seemed ashamed that his son danced, like he didn't want anyone to know."

I looked at George's face. Her cheeks were bright red, and there was fire behind her narrowed eyes. It was rare to see George this angry. She was one of the most levelheaded people I knew, and she prided herself on her ability to make logical decisions without letting her feelings get in the way. Bess was the opposite. Extremely empathetic, her feelings dictated almost every decision she made. I was less emotional than Bess and more emotional than George, and having both perspectives had led to many detective breakthroughs. I knew George had been upset seeing Michael yell at Colin, but I hadn't realized just how angry it had made her.

"You're right," I said. "But the vandalized poster seemed targeted at Maggie. Colin's name wasn't even crossed out," I pointed out.

"Michael didn't become the CEO of a major company by being dumb," George countered. "Crossing out Maggie's face makes the posters unusable, guaranteeing that a smaller audience will see his son dance. It also keeps the suspicion away from him. He's worth investigating," she insisted. "As CEO, he had access to the poster file, *and* he has a grudge against this ballet. Besides, do we have any better suspects?"

I wasn't sure that Mr. Carter would travel to River Heights just to sabotage a poster, but if I had learned anything over the years, it was that every lead, no matter how unlikely, was worth following. Even if the person didn't end up being the culprit, they often led to new information about the correct suspect.

"All right, " I said. "Let's talk to Michael."

"First we have to find him," George noted.

"Yeah, but we know he's from out of town, and it didn't seem like he was planning on leaving without Colin. . . ."

"So he must be checked into a hotel," George finished.

"Exactly," I said.

"Hang on," George said, whipping off her gloves and quickly typing on her phone. I knew exactly what she was doing. We'd searched for a suspect on an earlier case by visiting local hotels and asking for guests. "If you remember, there are eight hotels in River Heights," she said holding up her phone, showing me the list.

"All right," I said. "But let's call first this time. I have an idea. . . ."

George grinned widely as she dialed and handed me the phone. "Yes! Nancy Drew undercover. My favorite. Who are you going to pretend to be?"

I just smiled and wiggled my eyebrows in response. "You'll see."

"Hello and thank you for calling the River Heights Inn," a woman answered. "This is Karen. How may I help you?"

I took a deep breath. "Hi," I said in my most mature and authoritative voice. "My husband, Michael Carter, is on a business trip in River Heights, and I forgot where he's staying."

I heard Karen take a breath, as if she wanted to

say something, but I just kept right on going.

"I tried his cell phone, but it goes straight to voice mail. He probably forgot to charge it. Does your husband forget to charge his phone too?"

"I'm sorry," Karen interjected. "We can't give out—" I knew she was going to say that she couldn't give out guest information, but I didn't give her the chance. I kept talking, going even faster now.

"It is absolutely imperative that I reach him. Our cat is stuck in the chimney again. The dog chases her and she panics and she wedges herself up into the chimney. And Marmalade—that's our cat—she loves Michael. She'll come out if she hears his voice. I need to get him on the phone and put him on speaker. If I can't reach him, she'll stay up there for days . . . with no food, no water. I just don't know what will happen to her," I finished dramatically.

There was a pause on the other end of the line, and then I heard clicking sounds as Karen typed into the computer. I gave George a thumbs-up. My ruse had worked. George grinned.

"I'm sorry, Mrs. Carter," Karen said. "Your husband is not a guest at our hotel."

I hung up and turned back toward George. "One down. Seven to go," I said. George dialed the next number and I cleared my throat. When the clerk answered, I launched right in. "Hi, I believe my husband, Michael Carter, is a guest at your hotel. I simply must reach him. Our cat is stuck in the chimney. . . ."

It turned out Michael was staying at the fifth hotel we called: the Grand Hotel. As we drove over, I called Bess to update her and put her on speaker. I quickly ran through everything that had transpired since we'd split up.

"Anything happen at rehearsal we should know about?" I asked.

"No. I haven't let Fiona out of my sight, and nothing fishy has happened. Everyone has been focused on the show."

I heard Jamison screaming in the background. "Sarah, my ninety-year-old grandmother has better pointe work than that! You are a disgrace to this art form!"

"Man," George said. "He is really mean."

"No kidding," Bess said. "He's been yelling like that all afternoon. I've seen at least four dancers cry."

"Maybe it's just because of the stress he's feeling with Oscar LeVigne coming to the show," I said, trying to give Jamison the benefit of the doubt.

"I don't know," Bess said. "I've been talking some more with that guy, Sebastian, the pianist—"

"Do you have a crush on him?" George piped up. I grinned. I had been wondering the same thing. Bess is pretty and kind, and more or less every boy she meets ends up having a crush on her, but she's picky about who she'll go out with. Still, there was something about her voice that made me wonder if she was actually interested.

"What!? No!" Bess squawked. "He's just nice. Besides, I'm pretty sure he and Maggie are dating. Anyway, Sebastian says this is par for the course. Jamison always yells at the dancers."

I shook my head. "I can't imagine trying to solve a case with someone screaming at me to solve it faster. How does Jamison think this will make them dance better?"

"I don't know," Bess said. "I will say, though, he seems to get results. I think the ballet is going to be amazing."

"Well," George said, "I don't regret choosing robotics class over ballet."

"And I don't regret quitting ballet," I added.

We pulled into the hotel parking lot.

"We'll call you after we talk to Michael," I told Bess.

As I turned off the ignition, I turned to George. "You remember the plan?" I asked.

"It's not brain surgery," she said. "I wait precisely three minutes and then come in."

When I walked into the hotel, I spotted Michael in the lobby, reading a newspaper. I hadn't expected finding him to be so easy.

I straightened my sweater and approached him.

"Excuse me," I said. "Are you Michael Carter?"

He looked up at me, surprised. "Yeah, but call me Mike," he said. "And you are?"

"Nancy Drew," I introduced myself, extending my hand. "I'm the president of my school's Future Business Leaders of America. We have to do a report on a successful business in our state, and I picked Sharp Image."

A slow smile spread over Mike's face, and he straightened in his chair.

"Is that so?" he asked.

I nodded earnestly. "I was wondering if I could ask you a few questions."

"Sure, I don't see why not," Mike answered.

"Great." I pulled out my notebook. "Could you tell me how you got the idea to start Sharp Image?"

"Well, it all started in college, when I had to turn in a paper on Monet for an art history class. We had to include pictures of the paintings. . . ."

Mike kept talking, but I wasn't paying attention to his words. Instead I stared at his face. This past summer

I had studied a book on how to read facial expressions. It turns out there are tons of facial muscles that move unconsciously. Expressions flit across our face in microseconds, revealing our true emotions before we can consciously change our appearance. There are even police departments that employ people who can read faces in order to help determine when suspects are lying. They call them human lie detectors. I had been practicing on George, Bess, Ned, and even my dad for the past couple of months, but this was my first chance to try it during an actual case.

The book I read, written by the scientist who pioneered the research, suggested that once you have a sense of your subject's basic facial movements, you needed to catch them off guard. Surprising someone gives you the best chance of catching a micro-expression.

George walked in right on time. She found the hotel worker closest to Mike and me and strode up to her confidently.

"Hi," George said loud enough that Mike and I could hear her. "I'm helping the ballet company that's in town to perform." Mike's head whipped around, but I didn't take my eyes off his face. His eyebrows sank in and the muscles around his eyes tightened—a classic fear response.

"I was wondering if I could hang this poster for their upcoming performance in your lobby," George continued. "We think your guests may want to attend the show."

I kept staring at Mike. If he were paying attention to me, he'd probably think I was being extremely creepy, but his entire focus was on George. His mouth twitched as his teeth clenched and his cheeks sucked in.

"Unfortunately," the hotel clerk told George, "we have a no-advertising policy in our lobby."

"Oh, that's too bad," George said. "Thanks for your time." She exited the hotel.

Next to me, Mike's entire body relaxed. The hotel clerk noticed Mike and approached us.

"Mr. Carter?" she said. Mike looked up at her nervously. George had definitely caught him off guard with the poster. "Is your cat okay?"

"What?" Mike said loudly.

"Your wife called about your cat being stuck in the chimney. Were you able to talk her out of there?"

"But I don't have a cat," Mike said with a look of surprise.

"Oh, I must have been mistaken," the hotel clerk said.

"Excuse me," I said, standing up quickly. "I have an appointment I need to get to." I didn't want to stay around too long in case Mike figured out that a nosy girl had come in asking him questions not long after someone called claiming to be his wife. Sometimes being a detective is all about knowing when to make your exit.

As soon as I set foot outside, George accosted me.

"What did his expressions tell you?"

"I don't think he's our guy," I said.

George's face fell in disappointment. "Are you sure?"

"Well, it's an inexact science, and when he saw the poster he was definitely angry and embarrassed, but I didn't see anything that indicated that he was surprised or shocked that you would be asking to hang it, which he would have been if he knew it had been defaced."

"Darn it," George said, pounding her fist into her thigh. "I really wanted it to be him."

"I know," I said.

Just then my phone rang. It was Bess.

"Nancy!" she said breathlessly as soon as I answered. "You have to get back to the theater right away. Something horrible has happened!"

CHAPTER FIVE

Threatened

I PULLED UP IN FRONT OF THE THEATER, where Bess was pacing back and forth nervously. She yanked my car door open before I had even turned off the engine.

"Nancy! Thank goodness you're here. I don't know how I let this happen."

"Bess, slow down," I urged as I switched off the ignition and unbuckled my seat belt. "Just tell me everything."

Bess paused, as if she were searching for the right words. "I think I'd rather show you."

George and I followed Bess back into the theater. We walked quickly through the lobby, where clusters of dancers were whispering among themselves. They all looked shaken up.

We entered the auditorium, which was almost completely empty. Only Jamison sat in the front row, staring at the empty stage, seemingly lost in thought.

Bess indicated we should be quiet. I nodded. Based on what we'd heard earlier, I had no doubt Jamison would bite our heads off if we disturbed him.

We tiptoed past him and entered a door to the right that led backstage. The difference between what the audience sees onstage and what actually happens backstage never ceases to amaze me. It's part of what made me want to study ballet in the first place. When I was five, I saw *The Nutcracker* performed at that very theater. The daughter of one of Bess's mom's best friends was playing Clara, the lead, so we all got to go backstage after the performance. While we were watching the show, I had been completely captivated, transported to the Land of Sweets. But backstage I saw the pulleys that controlled the curtains, the painted back-drop that I had believed was a magical kingdom, and the costumes. For some people, seeing how the magic was made might have ruined the experience, but for me, seeing all the work that went into a production made it all the more impressive.

When I got home that day, I told my dad I wanted to take ballet. As much as I wanted to learn how to dance, I also wanted to learn how to put on a show. I like knowing how things work and seeing behind the scenes. It's part of what I enjoy about being a detective. Every person is putting on a show of some kind, projecting an image into the world. As a detective, you get to see behind that mask. You see what makes a person tick, who they really are.

Bess led us through another door, farther into the theater. The hallway was brightly lit with fluorescents and lined with doors whose signs read COSTUME SHOP, PROPS, and WORKSHOP.

Finally Bess stopped in front of a door marked LILAC FAIRY DRESSING ROOM and knocked on the door.

"Come in," Maggie said from the other side.

As soon as the door swung open, my jaw dropped. The entire room had been destroyed. All of Maggie's belongings—her makeup, her brush, her phone, her clothes—had been thrown on the ground and stomped on. The lightbulbs lining the mirror were shattered. The mirror itself sported a long crack right through the middle. One of a chair's legs had been broken off.

Maggie sat crumpled in the far corner of the room, as if she was trying to stay as far away from the chaos as possible.

"It looks like a hurricane came through here," George said.

"I take it back, Nancy," Maggie said, looking up at me, tears streaming down her face. "I want you to catch Fiona red-handed. She needs to be stopped!"

"We'll nab whoever did this!" I told Maggie. "You have my word."

"Mine, too," George said.

Next to me Bess cleared her throat. We all turned to look at her.

"The thing is," she started, "I kept a close eye on Fiona all afternoon. She never left my sight for more than a few seconds. There's no way she had time to do all of this," she said, swinging her arm out to take in the full dressing room.

A loud sob erupted from Maggie. "You mean we have no idea who did this?"

It was closer to the truth than I wanted to admit. The poster hadn't turned up anything, and with Bess ruling out Fiona, I was at a loss. Looking at Maggie, though, I couldn't say that out loud.

"Just because Fiona didn't do this herself," I said, "doesn't mean she wasn't behind it." Maggie looked up with a glimmer of hope on her tear-streaked face. "It's been a long day," I continued. "Why don't we go to dinner and you can give us a rundown of Fiona's friends who might have helped her."

Maggie nodded. "That sounds good." She quickly changed into her street clothes and we headed out.

Sebastian was sitting on a chair in the lobby, but he jumped up as soon as he saw Maggie.

"Maggie! Are you okay? I heard what happened." He came close as if he were going to hug her, but held back. I saw Bess smile. She loves couples. I think she was more excited when Ned and I started dating than either Ned or I were.

"I'm fine." Maggie sighed. "We were actually all going to grab dinner. Do you want to come?"

"I'd love to," Sebastian answered, following as we all headed out into the cold.

By the time our entrées arrived, Maggie was noticeably calmer. We'd decided to go to Hugo's Restaurant, much to George's chagrin. George is a burger and fries girl, and Hugo's specializes in organic health food. Maggie explained she was on a strict diet. She ate a lot of calories because of how much she exercised, but they were all healthy calories. It was imperative that she maintain her slim figure if she was going to have any shot at becoming a professional dancer.

George had been shocked when she found out all the things Maggie didn't eat: pizza, ice cream, steaks.

She couldn't believe that anyone would voluntarily not eat ice cream.

"Evelyn Young and Nicole Rush," Maggie said. "Those are Fiona's best 'friends.' I say friends, but they're more like lapdogs. They would do anything for her."

"Great," I said. "I'll focus my investigation on them tomorrow." I turned to Bess. "Can you just walk me through this afternoon one more time? I know you were focused on Fiona, but did anyone leave the rehearsal for a prolonged period of time?"

Before Bess could answer, Sebastian returned from the bathroom. "You guys are still talking about the dressing room? I thought the point of coming here was to give Maggie a break, get her mind off things," he said. "She needs to relax so she can get a good night's sleep tonight and be ready for tomorrow."

I was going to protest that I needed all the information I could get to solve this case before the performance. I had less than twenty-four hours, and we'd made very little headway so far.

But looking over at Maggie and seeing how distraught she was, I realized Sebastian was right. We weren't going to solve the case at the restaurant, and belaboring all the details wouldn't help Maggie do her best tomorrow.

I turned to Sebastian. "All right," I said. "Tell us about you. You seem really young to be the pianist for the tour."

Sebastian finished chewing a bite of his salmon salad. "Well, my sister, Veronica, is a ballet dancer too."

"She's not just a ballet dancer," Maggie added. "She's a member of the New York City Ballet—Jamison's only student to get into the company. Veronica is pretty much my idol."

"Right," Sebastian said. "What she said. When we were young, my parents decided we should practice together, make sure we kept each other honest about how much time we put in. She'd dance while I played. By the time I was eleven, I was accompanying all her recitals, and when I was fourteen the school started paying me to play for classes and performances, so I've basically been doing it for most of my life."

"That's incredible," Bess said.

"Hey," Maggie said to Sebastian. "Have you heard from Veronica recently?"

Sebastian shrugged. "I guess."

"I've been e-mailing, calling, texting. She never answers. What's up with that?"

Sebastian fidgeted with his napkin and took a big sip of his water. "Well, you know, she's a pro now. She's busy."

"Too busy to text her old friend?"

Sebastian shrugged again. "I don't know."

"Or does she not want to slum it with her amateur friends anymore?" Maggie said, visibly irritated.

"I thought we agreed not to discuss Veronica," Sebastian said quietly.

"So," Bess said, desperate to change the subject before it got any more tense, "how did you two get together?"

Sebastian and Maggie whipped their heads toward Bess in shock. Then they started laughing.

"No, no, no, no," Maggie said. "Sebastian's like my brother. I spent almost as much time at his house practicing with him and Veronica as I did my own."

"Yeah, we're just really good friends," Sebastian confirmed.

Bess blushed bright red. "Oh, I'm sorry! It's just that with the way you interact, I thought you were a couple."

"It's okay," Maggie said. "It happens all the time. We were even called into Jamison's office about it once."

"What do you mean?" George asked.

"The school doesn't allow students to be in relationships," Maggie said.

"They kick out dancers if they're caught breaking the rule," Sebastian explained.

"Seriously?" George asked.

Maggie shrugged. "Relationships are a distraction, and if you want to be a professional dancer, you can't afford any distractions."

I wasn't sure I agreed with that. Ned had helped me solve many mysteries. Sometimes if I was at a dead end and convinced that I wouldn't be able to solve a case, it was Ned who gave me the confidence to keep going. He never asked me to choose between him and sleuthing, and I had never considered him a distraction. If anything, he was an asset to helping me achieve my dreams.

"It takes so much discipline to be a professional dancer," George observed. "No ice cream, no boyfriends, and I bet you don't have a lot of time to play video games."

"Nope, none," Maggie confirmed with a smile.

"Yep, there's no way I could ever do that," George said, pulling her portable game system from her pocket and kissing it.

"It's definitely hard," Maggie agreed. "You sacrifice a lot, but when I'm on that stage, it's an amazing feeling. Last year in a recital I danced a pas de deux—that means dance of two—from *Swan Lake*. Colin danced the part of prince and I was Odile, the evil swan, distracting him from Odette, the swan princess. And as I danced, nothing else existed; nothing else mattered. When the music stopped and the audience clapped, I literally jumped. I had forgotten they were there! For the five minutes of my solo, I was completely transported to a snowy kingdom. It's a feeling I've never had doing anything else, and when I have it I know I've danced to the peak of my abilities."

"I can get like that when I'm writing a computer program," George said. "I just get so lost in the code that I lose complete track of time."

"Yeah," I agreed. "I feel that when I'm on a case and all the pieces start fitting together."

"It happens to me when I play piano," Sebastian concurred. "I think it's something you feel when you're doing something you're meant to do."

"I don't think I've ever felt that," Bess said sadly.

"You will," I said.

The server brought over our bill. "Whenever you're ready," he said, placing it on the table.

Maggie reached for it first. As she lifted the check off the tray, her face turned white.

"Nancy . . . ," she said.

I leaned over. On the tray under the bill was a note.

*FOR YOUR OWN SAKE, DON'T
DANCE TOMORROW!*

CHAPTER SIX

~∞~

Dashing Through the Snow

I SCANNED THE RESTAURANT AND SPOTTED our waiter, Chuck, in the back corner at the register.

"I'll be right back," I said, quickly pushing out of my chair and hurrying toward him.

"Excuse me," I said. "We found—"

Chuck didn't let me finish. "If there's something wrong with your food, you have to complain *before* you get your bill. We can't give discounts after we deliver the check," he said without looking up.

I shook my head. "Our food was fine," I corrected him. "We found a rude note under our bill."

"It wasn't from me," he said.

"I didn't think it was from you," I said with a frustrated sigh. "But did you see anyone handle our bill before you delivered it to us?"

"Nope," Chuck said, still not looking up from the register. I wasn't even sure he knew what I was asking. He was just trying to get me to leave him alone as soon as possible.

I put my hand on his shoulder, shaking it gently. He looked up at me, clearly annoyed. "Can you please just think about it for two seconds?" I asked firmly.

"Look, I'm sorry someone left you a mean note and hurt your feelings," he said, irritated, "but I need to put in this order for that big group over there." He pointed to a large party in the middle of the room. "They order a lot more food and give me a much bigger tip than you dancers with your kale salads and waters."

"No one at our table ordered a kale salad," I said.

"Sorry, I must have mixed up the tables of ballet dancers," Chuck said sarcastically.

"There was another table with a dancer?" I asked.

"Well, she was wearing the same sweatshirt as your friend that said 'Sleeping Beauty Ballet Regional Tour' on it, so I assume so. She was at a table with her father," Chuck said.

Adrenaline surged through my body as I quickly scanned the restaurant for another dancer. It was a cavernous space, with high-backed booths, which made it impossible to see who was sitting at half the tables.

"Where are they?" I asked Chuck urgently.

"At this point, I'm pretty sure I've gone above and beyond good customer service," Chuck said, his eyebrows arching pointedly.

"We'll tip twenty-five percent," I said. "That's well above the standard."

"Thirty percent," Chuck countered.

I took a deep breath. A large part of me wanted to tell this guy to kiss off into the sunset, but I couldn't afford to lose a case because I was too proud to negotiate with an annoying waiter.

"Fine," I said.

"They're right over there," he said, pointing to an empty table.

"Where?" I asked, louder than I meant to. A few of the tables closest to us turned to look at me, but I didn't care.

"Oh," Chuck said with a shrug. "I guess they left."

I pushed past him to the back door.

"Don't forget," Chuck called after me. "Thirty percent!"

"Yeah, yeah," I muttered under my breath as I stepped into the parking lot. I wasn't wearing my coat, and the icy air hit me like a brick wall, cutting straight through my sweater. I wrapped my arms around myself in a vain attempt to stay warm as I surveyed the parking lot.

A family—mom, dad, a girl, and a boy—was walking into the restaurant and an elderly couple was walking to their car, but I didn't see anyone from the ballet company.

"Where's your coat, dear?" the mom asked me. "You're going to get sick."

"It's inside," I said, thinking quickly. "The girl at the table next to me forgot her cell phone"—I held up my own phone—"so I ran out here to see if I could catch her, but I don't see her."

"Was the girl about your age?" the mom asked.

"Yes," I said. "And she was with her dad."

"Oh!" the mom said. "I think we parked right next to them. Last row, on the right. It's a black SUV."

"It's a Honda CR-V," the boy said. "That's barely an SUV. An SUV is more like a Land Rover or a Lexus LX."

The mom smiled at me apologetically. "Brad's obsessed with cars."

"Thanks for the info, Brad," I said with a smile. "I'm going to see if I can catch her. I know what it's like to lose a cell phone: it's no fun!"

I hurried deeper into the parking lot, weaving my way through rows of cars. My teeth chattered and my breath fogged up the air every time I exhaled. Just as I rounded the last row, a car headed toward the exit. It was a black Honda CR-V, just as Brad had described, but it was going away from me, so I couldn't see who was driving it, let alone the passenger.

The parking lot exit was far away from where I stood, but if I cut through the landscaping I could get there quickly. Maybe even quick enough to see who was in the car before it turned onto the street. The only obstacle was the pile of snow that had been plowed and pushed to the side, creating an eighteen-inch layer of the white stuff.

I took a deep breath and plunged my feet into the snow with a satisfying crunch. That satisfaction was short-lived as I felt the freezing water work its way into my shoes and drench my pants all the way to my knees. It took effort to lift each foot out and step again; it reminded me of running through tires in gym class, but much, much colder.

I continued on as fast as I could. Ahead of me, I saw the Honda at the exit, its left turn signal on. I could see the silhouette of what looked like a girl in the passenger seat, but because of the tinted window, I couldn't make out her face. I checked the street. The traffic was heavy at the moment, but a few hundred feet away the light was about to change to red, which would allow the driver to turn. I didn't have much time.

I pushed myself to move faster. In my head I could hear Ms. Brown, our PE teacher, yelling, "High knees, high knees" as I made my way through the snow. My toes were numb, and muscles I didn't even know existed burned in my legs.

Just a few more feet and I'd be close enough to see inside. My lungs screamed in pain. Tears ran down my face from the wind. I got there right as the car turned, and managed to make out the driver's face. It was Mike Carter! I still couldn't see who the passenger was, though.

When I walked back into the restaurant, I must have looked like a mess. I was shivering, my cheeks were bright red and tear-streaked, and I was drenched from the knees down.

"Nancy!" Bess shrieked, running over to me. "Are you okay?"

"I'm fine," I said. "I actually got a lead, but I'm not sure it makes sense."

"What is it?" George asked.

"No," Bess said. "Before we do any more investigating, we need to get you into dry clothes. You could get hypothermia!"

"We're close to the hotel. Sebastian and I need to get back for curfew, and I could lend you some dry clothes," Maggie said.

"The hotel is a lot closer than your house," George confirmed.

"Sounds good," I agreed.

Bess held out her hand.

"What?" I asked.

"You're not driving," she said. I wavered for a second, about to protest, but the look on Bess's face told me arguing would be pointless. I handed her the key.

Once we were in the car, Bess turned up the heat

full blast. I could see sweat beading on everyone else's foreheads, but I was grateful for the warmth. In a few minutes, I had stopped shivering and feeling had returned to my toes.

"The waiter said he saw another dancer and her father in the restaurant," I told them. "I followed the car and it was Mike Carter with a girl, but I couldn't see her face."

"I knew that guy was up to no good," George said.

"Yeah, but who was he with?" I asked. "Does Colin have a sister?"

"No," Maggie answered. "Colin's an only child. And why would Mike care if I dance tomorrow? He just doesn't want Colin to dance."

"Maybe he thinks that Jamison will cancel the show if you're not dancing, rather than let Oscar see an inferior performance."

Maggie shook her head. "There's no way. Jamison would never, ever cancel a performance."

"She's right," Sebastian added. "The phrase 'the show must go on' is just as important in ballet as it is in theater. Jamison would never work again if he canceled a performance for anything short of a major catastrophe, like an earthquake."

Sebastian leaned forward so he was speaking directly to me. "Look, Nancy," he said, "don't take this the wrong way, but I'm not sure you have the knowledge to solve this case."

"Nancy's solved cases that are loads harder than this," George said angrily.

"That's not what I meant," Sebastian said. "I'm sure you're a great detective, but ballet is a unique and insular world. I don't think anyone who isn't a part of it can solve a mystery about it."

"I disagree," I said, trying not to sound defensive. "My job as a detective is to ask questions and follow leads. As an outsider, sometimes you can spot inconsistencies that those immersed in a certain world could miss."

Sebastian shrugged. "All I'm saying, Maggie, is that maybe it's not worth the risk. Maybe you should let Fiona dance tomorrow."

Maggie looked at him as if he had just sprouted a unicorn horn in the middle of his forehead. "You think I should sit out dancing for Oscar LeVigne? Have you completely lost your mind?"

"There will be other opportunities to dance for Oscar. You're incredibly talented. What if you're so nervous that you dance badly? Or even injure yourself? That would be worse than not dancing for him at all. Oscar gives you one shot; you don't want to blow it."

"I hate to admit it," Bess said, "but I understand what he's saying. I know you can solve this case, Nancy, but we don't have a lot of time, and the stakes for Maggie are really high."

"No," Maggie said firmly. "I'm performing for Oscar tomorrow. As a dancer, my potential career is already short. I'll be considered old by the time I'm thirty, so I can't afford to waste any time. Besides, I earned this opportunity. I'm going to take it."

We pulled up to the hotel and Bess parked.

"So what's the plan?" Maggie asked as we rode the

elevator to the twelfth floor. "How are you going to solve this?"

I didn't answer right away. I could tell my hesitation was making Maggie nervous, but the truth was that I was stuck. I needed to think about my next move. I mentally ran through my day—how we'd gone from the copy shop to Mike's hotel—and realized Sebastian was right. Ballet was its own world, and I had been outside that world. I had been chasing down clues on the periphery, but if I was going to solve this case, I needed to be in the thick of it.

"You know how Jamison scheduled a rehearsal tomorrow before the performance?" I asked.

Maggie nodded.

"Well, George, Bess, and I will be there."

"We will?" George asked, her face turning pale.

"It's a closed rehearsal," Sebastian said. "That means only company members can attend."

"Well, company members and Miss Taylor's ballet class," I said with a smile.

CHAPTER SEVEN

Too Many Suspects

"ALL RIGHT, NANCY," MAGGIE SAID. "LET'S see what you remember. Show me first position."

I slid my heels together and turned out my toes, making my feet as close to horizontal as I could. Maggie raised her eyebrows. "Not bad. Your turnout is pretty good!"

"Thanks," I said. "I'm glad I still have some of my old skills."

"Okay, let's keep going. We have a lot to cover in the next hour. Second position," she said.

I slid my heels about a foot apart, keeping my toes turned out.

"Good. Now third."

We kept going like that, working through standard barre warm-ups and some basic jumps and turns, including jetés, *piqués*, and fouettés. I wouldn't say it was like riding a bike, where it comes back easily if you haven't done it in a while, but I was surprised at how familiar the old movements felt. Instinctually, I could feel my arms knowing how to hold themselves and my neck moving into alignment with my spine to create an elegant line.

I had just finished a set of jumps across the floor when Bess and George walked in. I'd only been at it an hour, but I could already tell I'd be sore tomorrow.

"I hate to say it, because you know I have faith in you, Nancy, but any chance you have a plan B?" George asked with a grin. "You're not exactly looking like a prima ballerina."

She was wearing all black, like the stage crew members. Bess wore the same outfit that the theater ushers wore. Even she couldn't help chuckling when she saw me in my tights and tutu, panting, sweat running down my face, my hair falling out of its bun.

"I just need Jamison and the other members to think I'm one of Miss Taylor's students, and Miss Taylor's students to think I'm part of the company," I explained. "No one needs to think I'm a future star. In fact, the more I blend in, the more chances I'll get to observe the other dancers, overhear their conversations, and keep an eye on Maggie."

Maggie nodded. "Stay in the back, do your best to find the gaps in the light, so you're in the dark, and just watch whoever goes before you very carefully."

"Got it," I said. I checked my watch. Rehearsal would officially begin in about ten minutes. "I'm going to do my hair and makeup."

Maggie nodded. "I'm going to freshen up too."

"Remember," I said, "when you see me out there, you don't know me."

Maggie waved good-bye and headed backstage to the dressing rooms. She looked small and nervous as she walked away. I wished I could have done more to reassure her.

Bess, George, and I headed to the ladies' room. Once inside, I locked the door.

"Bess," I asked, "can you help me with my makeup? You're so much better at it than I am."

"Sure," Bess said. "What do you want?"

"Heavy eye makeup. I'm hoping that with that and my hair in a bun, no one will recognize me."

"Got it," Bess said, getting to work.

"What are our marching orders?" George asked.

"Just keep your eyes open for anything that looks weird or out of place."

"You bet," George said. "If we see something, we'll say something."

"Between all of our eyes, I doubt whoever is doing this will be able to get away with it," I said.

I could hear a bunch of girls walking through the lobby, chattering with one another. Butterflies flooded my stomach. I had gone undercover several times before, but I still became nervous every time. I guess it wasn't that different from Maggie's stage fright. Going undercover is a type of performance.

Bess noticed the wide-eyed, panicked look on my face.

"You can do this, Nancy," she said.

"You definitely can," George said.

"If I look like I'm really flailing out there, turn out the lights," I told George.

"I'm on it," she said with a grin.

I smiled, happy to have my friends' support. Knowing that they had my back made me breathe a little easier.

"All done," Bess said. I looked in the mirror. Bess had done an amazing job. I looked like a real ballet dancer, my hair pulled tightly into a bun, my eyes wide and dark. Some of my usual confidence returned.

"All right," I said. "Eight hours until show time. Let's find whoever's doing this to Maggie."

I made it through the warm-up exercises with little trouble. The nice thing was that barre warm-up is always the same whether you're in an intermediate class or a professional. It still felt familiar, and I was able to follow along, which allowed me to observe the people around me. You really could tell a lot about a person from how they danced. For instance, Colin's movements seemed full of rage, while Fiona moved selfishly, as if she were the only person in the room with no regard for the people around her.

As we lined up for floor work, I managed to slide in behind Evelyn and Nicole, Fiona's friends, whom Maggie had pointed out earlier. I could hear them whispering, but I couldn't make out what they were saying. I inched closer as Maggie leaped across the stage and noticed Evelyn roll her eyes.

"Someone tell her Oscar's not here yet," she whispered. "Seriously, she doesn't have to try so hard."

"I can't wait for someone to take her down a notch," Nicole agreed.

"Yeah, like yesterday," Evelyn said. Nicole smiled, and they exchanged a conspiratorial look.

Nicole was about to say something when she noticed

me staring. "Ever hear of personal space?" she asked, glowering.

"Sorry," I said. "I couldn't help overhearing. What happened yesterday?"

Evelyn gave me a dismissive once-over. "Nothing an amateur like you needs to worry about."

"Is that chitchat I hear?" Jamison bellowed from below us. "If I hear another peep, we start from the top, and you can blame Chatty Kathys over there." Nicole glared at me, as if I had been the only one talking. No one said anything for the rest of warm-ups.

Before I knew it, though, an hour had gone by. We had a ten-minute break before rehearsal officially began. Backstage I spotted Fiona by herself, anxiously digging through her purse.

"Hi," I said as I approached her. "I'm in Miss Taylor's class. It's such an honor to dance with you today."

"Thanks," Fiona said, barely looking up from her purse.

"I was watching you during warm-ups. You have

an incredible line. What part are you dancing?"

"I'm the understudy for the Lilac Fairy," she replied.

"Understudy!?" I squawked. "I can't believe someone as good as you is an understudy."

"Yeah, well, sometimes life isn't fair," she said.

"Who's dancing instead of you?" I asked.

"Maggie Richards," she said.

"The girl in the first row on the right?" I asked. Fiona nodded.

"She's good," I said, "but not nearly as good as you." I hoped flattery would encourage her to confide in me.

Fiona stopped looking in her purse and looked up at me. I felt a tingle of excitement.

"You're an idiot," she said with a withering look. "Maggie Richards is phenomenally talented. She deserves the Lilac Fairy role. What I don't understand is why I didn't get another role. Instead I'm stuck understudying a difficult one."

It was all I could do to keep my mouth from hanging open in shock. I hadn't expected Fiona to say anything complimentary about Maggie at all.

"Argh," Fiona said, swinging her purse over her arm. "I must have left my phone in the dressing room. I have to go get it." She spun around with such force that her bag swung and slammed into her back. A piece of paper fluttered to the ground.

I reached down to pick it up. I was about to call out to Fiona when something caught my eye. It was a receipt for Hugo's. I checked the date and time stamp: last night at 7:37. Exactly when we had been there.

I hadn't noticed Fiona when I'd searched the restaurant, so she could have been the girl Chuck, the waiter, had seen with Mike Carter, but why would Fiona be spending time with Mike?

I felt like I was taking one step forward and two steps back with every clue. Nothing was adding up.

I couldn't think about it too long before it was time for rehearsal. Luckily, Jamison only wanted to work on select scenes, so I was able to float into the wings and avoid suspicion.

I paid close attention when Maggie danced her climactic solo. Just as I had back in Miss Taylor's class as a kid, I became lost watching her. There was something about her dancing that wouldn't let you look away. My reverie was disrupted when Jamison screamed, "No, no, no! You're doing it all wrong."

Maggie stopped abruptly. "Sorry—" she started to say, but Jamison interrupted her.

"The Lilac Fairy is supposed be light and dreamy. You're dancing it cold and tepid. What is wrong with you today?"

"Sorry," Maggie started again. "I'm just a little on edge."

"What did you say?" Jamison asked. His voice was quiet, but I could tell he was on the brink of exploding. All the other dancers had their heads down, not wanting to see what was going to happen, except Nicole and Evelyn, who watched with barely contained smirks.

Maggie gulped. She seemed to know she had made a mistake. I felt somebody come up behind me and turned around to find George.

"This isn't going to be good," she whispered under her breath.

I nodded in agreement.

"What. Did. You. Say?" Jamison repeated, this time with even more menace in his voice.

"I'm a little on edge," Maggie managed to squeak out. I saw her shoulders tense, as if she was literally bracing herself for what Jamison was going to do next.

"Do you want to be a professional dancer?" Jamison asked. "You do, don't you?"

Maggie nodded nervously.

"When you're a professional, do you know what your job is?"

Maggie nodded.

"Your job is to dance . . . PERFECTLY!" he bellowed. "It doesn't matter what's going on in your personal life. Your job is to dance the way every audience member in the theater—who have paid money to see you—wants to see you."

"Yes, sir," Maggie said, but Jamison had just gotten started.

"It doesn't matter if your boyfriend broke up with

you thirty minutes before curtain time. It doesn't matter if your grandmother is lying in a hospital bed. It doesn't matter if someone is threatening you or harassing you."

George and I exchanged a look. That was a weird thing to mention. Did Jamison know something about what was happening to Maggie?

"You want to be like Veronica, right? If I recall correctly, she's your idol."

Maggie nodded.

"Well, Veronica would be the first to tell you that being a professional dancer is no picnic. It's hard work, and you can never make excuses. Isn't that right, Sebastian?" he said.

Sebastian looked up from the piano and glared at Jamison. He didn't say anything.

"Isn't that right, Sebastian?" Jamison repeated. "Tell her how hard it is to be a professional dancer."

"It's really hard," he said quietly, never taking his eyes off Jamison. He looked furious.

"Sebastian's reacting really strongly," I observed to George.

"Maybe Bess is right. Maybe he's in love with Maggie," George said.

"And do professionals tolerate people making excuses?" Jamison continued to interrogate Sebastian.

The pianist shook his head.

"I can't hear you!" he yelled.

"No," Sebastian hissed.

"Thank you," Jamison said before turning back to Maggie. "I don't care what's going on with you. Suck it up and dance this part like I know you are capable of."

Maggie nodded. But instead of looking completely humiliated and downtrodden, she looked determined . . . and even inspired.

Something occurred to me, and I turned to George. "Do you think Jamison is the one harassing Maggie, as some sort of tough-love, inspirational thing?" I asked.

"I don't know," George answered. "Would he risk that when this performance means as much to him as it does to Maggie?"

I shrugged. It did seem like an odd choice, but Jamison was nothing if not eccentric. I gazed at the stage. "Look, though," I said. "Maggie is dancing better."

Bess came up behind us. "Guys," she whispered urgently, "I found something."

"What?" I asked.

She held out her phone and showed a picture of Colin drinking water in the lobby.

"How is this a clue?" I asked.

Bess took back the phone and zoomed in. "Look at his arms," she insisted.

I took the phone back and saw that Colin's arms were covered in cuts. There were bandages over some of them.

"I didn't notice any cuts on his arms when we saw him fighting with his dad yesterday, did you?" Bess asked.

I shook my head.

"Those definitely look like they could have come from a broken mirror," George said. "Like the one in Maggie's dressing room."

"They do," I agreed. "But what would Colin have against Maggie? Why wouldn't he want her to dance?"

"Maybe if he can't, she can't?" George suggested.

"But he's here," I pointed out. "He's dancing."

"That doesn't matter. He definitely stays on the suspect list," Bess said.

"So does Fiona," I said. I showed them the receipt. "And I heard Nicole and Evelyn talking about wanting to take Maggie down a notch."

"Plus, now you have this Jamison theory," George said. Bess looked at us, confused, and we quickly explained.

"Well, if it's him, then we know it's for Maggie's own good and we don't have to worry about her," George said.

"But if it's not him . . . ," Bess began.

I looked at the time on Bess's phone and sighed.

"We have only six hours until curtain and I'm still adding suspects. I need to be eliminating them," I lamented.

"How can we do that?" George asked.

I thought for a moment. Ordinarily, I would follow each clue and see where it led, methodically crossing out suspects, but I didn't have time for that.

"We need to set a trap," I announced.

~

CHAPTER EIGHT

Proof

DURING THE NEXT BREAK, GEORGE, BESS, and I cornered Maggie and filled her in on our plan.

"Are you sure about this?" Maggie asked nervously.

I nodded. "Everyone in the company knows that nerves are your greatest weakness. The culprit is probably preying on that," I said.

Maggie swallowed hard and averted her eyes.

I realized I had said the wrong thing. "Sorry," I said. "I didn't mean to be rude."

"It's okay," Maggie said. "You're not saying anything I don't know. Nerves have been my Achilles' heel since the first time I strapped on a pair of shoes. Once the lights go down, the curtain goes up, and I set foot on that stage, I'm fine. All the butterflies in my stomach, the nausea, the racing heart, go away in an instant. But right before I go onstage, it's a different story. It would be okay, except to get hired as a professional, they want to know that you're going to be able to dance. If you seem nervous, they don't want to hire you."

"I know what you mean," I said. "There are some cases that I'm not a hundred percent sure I can solve, but I have to act like I am. Otherwise my client won't trust me."

"Exactly," Maggie agreed.

"Do you have a lucky charm or anything?"

"Yeah," Maggie said. "When I got into the academy, my mom gave me a pair of Moira Devereux's shoes—the ones she wore when she debuted on the Covent Garden stage in London. She's one of the best ballet dancers in the world. I keep them with me at all times to remind me what I want to achieve."

"Do the other dancers here know about them?" I asked.

"Yeah, I take them out of their case and rub them for good luck before every performance. Everyone's seen me do it."

I took a deep breath. "I need to use them as bait," I said.

Maggie looked at me like I was crazy. "No," she said firmly. "I can't risk it. Too much has gone wrong already."

"I'll make sure they're safe. I won't let them out of my sight, but a trap is the only way to catch this culprit before the performance."

"I don't know . . . ," Maggie said.

"I wouldn't ask if there was another option," I said. "We're running out of time. If we don't force the culprit's hand, I might not be able to find out who it is before the show."

"She'll be careful," Bess assured her.

"Nancy's set traps before. She knows what she's doing," George added.

Maggie looked at all three of us. "You have to promise to treat them like they are made of pure gold. That's how valuable they are to me."

"I promise," I said.

Maggie went off to fetch the shoes.

"No pressure," I joked to Bess and George.

"It's worth the risk," Bess said.

"I know," I said. "I just wish it hadn't gotten to this point. I really thought this case would be easier."

"They're never easy," George pointed out.

"I think that's how you know what your 'thing' is," Bess said. "You keep doing it even when it's hard and frustrating."

"I can see that," I said. "No one likes every aspect of anything, so you have to find what you truly love despite the difficult parts."

"Yeah," George said. "Staring at a computer screen isn't the fun part about writing code, but I still like it ten times more than I'd like the best part of, say, dancing." She waved her arm around.

"Right," Bess said. "We've seen how difficult it is

to dance at Maggie's level, but she didn't even consider not performing tonight."

George and I nodded.

A few seconds later, Maggie returned with the shoes.

"Here they are," she said, holding out a pair of old red ballet shoes. "I know they don't look like much," she added, "but these shoes have danced some of the hardest roles on the world's best stages. I like to think of each crease as a badge of honor." She handed them to me. "Please, just be careful."

"Actually," I said, "I'm not going to set the trap. You are."

Maggie's eyes widened in surprise. "What do I have to do?"

I leaned over and whispered the plan into her ear.

A few minutes later, I was sitting in the back row of the theater, slouched down so that I remained out of view. I spied Fiona sitting in the front row, looking at her phone. Colin was in the aisle, stretching, and Jamison was, predictably, yelling at a group of dancers on the stage.

Maggie was in the corner, holding her shoes and tapping her foot anxiously. She looked over at me, and I nodded.

Slowly she made her way across the theater toward Sebastian, who was sitting at the piano.

Sebastian looked up at her. "Hey," he said. "How are you holding up?"

Maggie cleared her throat. "I'm okay," she said. Then she looked around the room before taking a deep breath. "I have a favor to ask you," she said loudly. "You know the shoes my mother gave me? The ones that used to belong to Moira Devereux that I use for good luck?"

She was practically shouting, and her delivery seemed stiff and awkward. I grimaced. Acting natural when undercover was always harder than people thought.

"Uh, yeah?" Sebastian said, confused.

Jamison shot Maggie an irritated glance, so at least I knew he was paying attention.

"With everything that's happened," she continued loudly, "I don't feel safe leaving them unattended."

She paused and looked around the room, then raised her voice even more. "You know that I can't dance if I don't touch them before the performance. If anything happened to them, I would be absolutely devastated." She was speaking so loudly by this point that the whole room was staring at her.

"Have you lost your mind?" Jamison snapped. "No one cares about your silly shoes. There's no such thing as a good-luck charm. You'd be better off without them."

"We'll see about that," I murmured under my breath.

Maggie ignored Jamieson. "Can I put my shoes in your piano bench?" she asked Sebastian, still loudly. "I'd just feel safer if I knew someone was keeping an eye on them."

"Sure," Sebastian said, still looking confused. He stood up and Maggie opened the bench, carefully placing the shoes inside.

"Thanks," Maggie said. "I really appreciate it. I know they'll be safe here," she added, pointedly looking around the room.

She headed back toward the stage and I checked out my suspects. Colin was staring at Maggie. Fiona was fixated on the bench. At first I thought Jamison didn't care at all, but I caught him giving the piano a furtive glance. They were all still contenders.

I pulled out my phone. NOW, I texted George.

A second later a fire alarm blared through the entire theater. Lights flashed over the theater exits. The dancers stopped in their tracks and covered their ears.

"You have GOT to be kidding me," Jamison screamed over the ringing. "We DO NOT have time for this." He threw down the papers he was holding. His face was bright red and a vein in his forehead pulsed in anger. I thought I had seen him mad before, but that seemed downright calm compared to the level of fury now emanating off him.

The dancers began exiting the building. "Where do you think you're going?" Jamison yelled.

"It's a fire alarm . . . ," Nicole began.

"Do you smell smoke? Do you see flames? Does it feel hot in here to you?" Jamison asked.

"No," Nicole said hesitantly.

"Then there's no fire! This is a false alarm. You will stay and you will prepare. We open in four hours."

My jaw dropped. I couldn't believe Jamison wouldn't allow his dancers to evacuate during a fire alarm. That had to be illegal. Not to mention my trap wasn't going to work if the theater stayed full. We needed to do something.

I scurried over to Bess. "Tell him he has to evacuate."

"What?" she said. I couldn't tell whether she couldn't hear me over the blaring alarm or she couldn't believe what I was asking.

"You have to tell him to evacuate!" I repeated, louder this time.

"Why me?"

"Because you look like you're part of the theater staff," I said. "He won't listen to me dressed like this." I indicated my leotard and tutu.

"He'll bite my head off," she said.

"Just stay firm."

Bess took a deep breath and marched toward

Jamison. "Sir," she said confidently. The alarm masked the nervous quiver I was sure was in her voice.

"Yes?" Jamison asked, feigning innocence.

"The law mandates that you evacuate during a fire alarm."

"There's no fire. This is just an annoyance. Please go back to sweeping or whatever chore you fill your day with."

Bess set her jaw defiantly. "If the fire department arrives and the building is not evacuated, they will issue a fine."

"Serves you right for having a faulty fire alarm. Imagine if it had gone off during a performance!" Jamison hissed.

Bess narrowed her eyes. "I will make sure they issue the fine directly to you personally. And I should add that it's quite hefty."

Jamison paused for a beat. Then, finally, "All right, everyone get your coats." He turned to Bess. "These are dancers. Their muscles need to stay warm."

If I hadn't been trying to maintain a low profile,

I would have jumped for joy. A sense of pride swelled through me. The first time Bess had gone undercover, she'd blushed and stuttered, and her cover had been blown in less than thirty seconds. She had come a long way since then.

As the dancers filed out of the room, I discreetly slid down between the seats and hid. The floor was cold and dirty. There are times when being a detective isn't really glamorous.

Finally the theater was empty. Now the real waiting began. If the culprit wanted to rattle Maggie, he or she would use this opportunity to steal her lucky ballet shoes. All I needed to do was catch him or her in the act.

My back ached from being curled up under the seat. It felt like I'd been in this position for hours, but I knew it was closer to ten minutes. My dad, a famous attorney in River Heights, had taught me that willpower is never enough; you have to help yourself succeed. If I dwelled on how much I wanted to move, I'd be doomed. I started reciting the capitals of all the states in my head for distraction.

I was trying to remember the capital of South Dakota when I heard the door to the theater open. I held my breath. I couldn't see who it was, but I didn't dare risk being seen by popping my head up. It wouldn't be definitive proof unless I caught the culprit holding the ballet shoes. I heard the intruder slowly tiptoe down the center aisle toward the piano bench.

Then there was a long pause. I was desperate to know what was happening, but I forced myself to wait. Finally I heard the piano bench creak loudly.

That was my cue. I sprang to my feet, my knees protesting in pain after being curled up on the floor for so long.

I spun around. Leaning over the piano bench, ballet shoes in hand, was Fiona!

~

CHAPTER NINE

A Surprising Discovery

"STOP RIGHT THERE," I SAID. I KNEW THAT as soon as everyone realized there wasn't actually a fire, they'd come streaming back into the theater.

"W-what are you doing in here?" Fiona stammered.

"Maggie asked me to investigate who was harassing her, and I just caught you in the act."

Fiona snorted. "That's so Maggie. You play a few pranks and she calls in a private detective. God, she is such a drama queen."

"I'd say someone trying to ruin her opportunity to dance in front of Oscar and steal her big break warrants some extreme measures," I said pointedly.

"You think I'm trying to dance in front of Oscar?" Fiona asked, horrified.

"Why else would you be harassing her" I asked.

"I wanted to dance *some* performances on this tour, so sure, I took her wig that one time and set up some fake wake-up calls, but I would die if I had to dance tonight. Oscar would eat me alive. I don't need to read about how *not* talented I am!"

"Then why did you install that app on her phone that made her late? You knew Jamison was going to bench her!" I countered.

"I didn't do that," Fiona said. "I admit that I always enjoy seeing Jamison yell at her, but I can barely figure out how to put a filter on a photo. I wouldn't even know what app to download to do what you're talking about."

Just then the door opened and dancers came pouring in, Jamison leading the way. He reminded me of the Pied Piper leading the children out of Hamelin.

"Everyone, back to your places!" he yelled. "We have wasted enough time."

Maggie, Bess, and George rushed over to Fiona and me.

"All right!" George cheered. "Your trap worked!"

I looked at Fiona, suddenly doubtful I had caught the right somebody.

Before I could say anything, though, Maggie snatched her shoes out of Fiona's hands. She looked so angry, I was worried she might slap Fiona.

"You're going to pay for this," Maggie hissed.

"I'm sorry I played some jokes on you, even though, really, you should be thanking me. You'll be hazed way worse when you join a professional company. I toughened you up, but whatever. I swear I'm not trying to ruin your performance for Oscar tonight."

"Then why did you sneak in here during the fire alarm to take Maggie's lucky shoes?" I asked.

Fiona looked around to make sure no one was watching, then leaned in closer.

"I wasn't trying to take the shoes. They were just in the way. I was trying to take this."

She reached into the piano bench and pulled out a strip of photos, the kind taken in the photo booths that you see at amusement parks or weddings.

These photos were of Fiona and Colin. In the first one, they smiled. In the second one, they stuck their tongues out. The third, they held bunny ears over each other's heads, and in the fourth they kissed.

Maggie's eyebrows shot to the top of her head, and her jaw literally dropped open. "You and Colin are together?" she asked, sounding completely scandalized.

"Shh!" Fiona hissed. "No one can know! I hid the photo strip in the piano bench. I was worried that you would find it when you went to get your shoes back, so I used the fire alarm as an opportunity to take them, but then your hired goon confronted me."

Suddenly a thought occurred to me. "Were you at Hugo's last night with Colin's dad?" I asked.

Fiona nodded. "But Colin wasn't." She looked at Maggie. "Please don't be mad at Colin," she said.

"Why would I be mad at Colin?" Maggie asked. "I *like* Colin."

"I know," Fiona said. "And he likes you. I don't even think it was really personal. He was just lashing out. You know how he gets when he's angry, and yesterday after his dad showed up and threatened to never let him dance again, he was so upset." Fiona looked down at the ground, fighting back tears. "He was saying how it wasn't fair. All your dreams were coming true with Oscar coming to the performance and everything, and all his dreams were being ruined."

It took a second to click into place, but I realized what she was saying. "Colin destroyed Maggie's dressing room, didn't he?" I asked.

Fiona nodded miserably. "It was so scary."

"I don't get it," Maggie asked. "I thought Colin and I were friends."

"You are. He was out of control. Your dressing room was just in the wrong place. I knew I had to do something to try to help him. I convinced his dad to meet for dinner. I wanted to persuade him to come to the show tonight. I thought if he saw Colin dance, he would realize how good Colin is, and maybe he'd change his mind."

She looked at the ground. "But I don't think I got through to him. He just kept saying how embarrassing it was to see his son in tights."

She took a deep breath. Tears leaked from her eyes and ran down her cheeks. She clearly cared a lot about Colin. I looked over at Maggie, whose face had softened.

"I know Colin's really sorry about your dressing room. He's planning on writing you a letter of apology, promising to pay for the damage."

Maggie nodded, obviously still trying to make sense of everything that Fiona had just said.

Fiona looked up at the stage. "Your scene is next. You'd better get to the wings before Jamison flips his lid."

"You're right," Maggie said. She hurried backstage, and Fiona followed her.

George, Bess, and I sat in some nearby seats.

"So," George said, "case closed? Whatever Fiona

didn't do was Colin acting out because of his dad?"

I thought about it. It certainly explained some of what had happened to Maggie, but not all of it. And, more importantly, it didn't feel right. I had learned to trust my instincts when it came to solving mysteries. Usually everything fit together, and there were no more niggling doubts in the back of my mind. I didn't have that feeling now. Colin destroying Maggie's room had been impulsive and irrational. Everything else that happened to Maggie—that is, other than the pranks Fiona had confessed to—had been planned out; there seemed to be a purpose behind it.

"I'm not sure," I said. "Maggie's phone being tampered with and the poster being vandalized all happened before Colin was confronted by his dad."

"Yeah," George said, "but it's not like Mike was ever supportive. I bet Colin's been jealous of Maggie and the support she gets for a long time."

I shook my head. "It just seems like a stretch. Besides, Colin wasn't even at the restaurant last night, so he couldn't have left the note."

"But Mike could have," George insisted.

"George," I said, "you're letting your personal dislike of Mike cloud your judgment. Mike seems really focused on Colin, and Fiona just confirmed that he hasn't even seen the show. I doubt he knows how important Maggie's role is."

"I guess," George said begrudgingly.

"He's still guilty of being a bad father," I said.

"Yeah," George said.

We sat in silence for a moment. "I just . . . ," I started, trying to figure out how to articulate my thoughts. "I feel like we're not thinking about this in the right way."

"What do you mean?" Bess asked.

"I don't know," I said. "In most cases, we don't have enough information, and it's a matter of collecting more clues in order for it to all make sense."

"But you don't feel that way about this one?" Bess asked.

I shook my head. "No. It feels like we have all the information we need, but we're not looking at it from the right angle. Like we have it upside down or sideways or something," I said.

"Okay," Bess said. "Why don't we go over everything we know and then see if we can make sense of it?"

"Yeah," George said. "I'll type it all up, and that way we can move the clues around to try to see them differently."

"Good idea!" I said.

George left to get her laptop from her bag backstage, then came back to sit next to us.

"Ready," she said, her hands poised over the keys.

"Okay," I began. "Let's go in the order we discovered the clues, so we don't forget anything."

"All right," Bess said. "Yesterday someone tampered with Maggie's phone to make her late for rehearsal."

"Right. Then a little after that we discovered that someone had vandalized the poster for the show, so that Maggie's picture was destroyed," I said.

"But," George put in, "given the timing of printing posters, that probably happened before the phone was tampered with. Should I put that above the phone on our timeline?"

"Yeah," I said. "That's a good idea."

"So, next—" Bess started, but she was interrupted by Jamison's voice echoing throughout the theater.

"You!" he boomed. "Corps de ballet! Get onstage." I froze as I waited for whoever he was yelling at to respond, but no one moved. "Hello! Corps de ballet! We are waiting." I looked around the theater as a horrifying realization dawned on me. No one else from Miss Taylor's class had returned from the fire drill. Jamison must have fully closed the rehearsal. It was just me.

Jamison marched up the aisle toward me. My mouth went dry and my hands started shaking as adrenaline surged through my body. This was it. He was going to blow my cover and kick me out, and I still didn't know who was after Maggie.

"Hello!?" he repeated. "Do I have a deaf dancer in my company that I didn't know about?"

He stared at me, awaiting my response. I looked up blankly. Did he actually believe that I was a member of this tour? Next to me Bess squeezed my hand. I took a deep breath. There was no way out. I was just going to have to muddle through the best I could.

"Sorry, sir," I said, pleasantly surprised by how confident my voice sounded. I had been sure it would come out a barely audible squeak. "I—"

"I don't want to hear any excuses. Get on the stage now," he roared. "You are holding up my rehearsal!"

I gave one last look at George and Bess, who nodded encouragingly, and scurried onto the stage. All the other corps de ballet members stared at me. I could hear whispers among the crowd. They, at least, realized I didn't belong.

It would be only a matter of moments before the whole jig was up. The music started and the rest of the corps de ballet glided out to their positions.

"Stop!" Jamison said. He looked right at me. "If you're so sure you don't need to rehearse that you can spend time gabbing, let's see you dance . . . alone. Everyone, clear the stage, please." The other corps de ballet members shuffled off to the wings, leaving me alone on the stage. I knew I was imagining it, but it felt like there was a giant spotlight directly on me.

"Sebastian!" Jamison barked. "Begin." He turned back to me. "All right, missy, let's see what you can do."

Sebastian started to play. I stepped into the center of the stage as I had seen the other members do earlier.

All of a sudden, there was a loud creaking noise above me. It sounded like something heavy was giving way. I looked up to see a giant tree, a prop and an essential element of the enchanted forest set, swaying ominously directly above me.

There was another cracking noise, this time louder than the last, and one side of the tree dropped dramatically, as if the cable holding it had snapped.

Acting purely out of instinct, I leaped out of the way, covering my head with my arms, just as another *crack* echoed through the theater, and the tree came crashing down onto the stage.

CHAPTER TEN

A Shift in Perspective

I KEPT MY HANDS OVER MY HEAD AND MY eyes shut until the crashing stopped. I could hear people screaming all around me.

"What on earth?" Jamison yelled. "What else can possibly go wrong?"

I was wondering the same thing as I quickly took stock of my body. I ached from hitting the stage as hard as I did, and a sharp, piercing pain was shooting through my right foot.

Slowly I opened my eyes. A dozen members of the corps de ballet, all in matching tutus, hovered over me. I felt like I was inside a kaleidoscope; I started to wonder if I had hit my head, too.

Before I could do anything, I felt an arm wrapping around my shoulder. I turned my head and saw a small but strong-looking woman next to me; her entire presence exuded calm. I immediately felt safe.

"I'm Linda, the medical trainer with the theater. Does anything hurt?"

"My foot . . . ," I started, reaching down to grab it. Now that the adrenaline was wearing off, the pain felt even more acute. "A piece of the set hit it. I think it might be broken," I said.

"Let's get you back to my office and we can take a look." She helped me up as I balanced on my good leg. "Can you put any weight on it?" Linda asked.

Gingerly, I tried to take a step, but the pain intensified and shot up my leg all the way to my knee. Tears sprang to my eyes.

"I don't think so," I said. I tried to stay calm, but I was already imagining trying to navigate around River Heights on crutches in the snow. Ned and I were supposed to go on a ski trip for Valentine's Day. Now who knew if I would be able to go?

Linda helped me down the hall to her office. I knew George and Bess would be following as soon as they could. Behind me, I heard Jamison bellowing at his dancers, telling them rehearsal was over and to go back to the hotel to rest before the show.

Inside her office, Linda helped me up onto the exam table. Before she could get started, Bess, George, and Maggie burst in. I was grateful to see them.

"Nancy! Are you okay?" Bess asked frantically.

"Are you hurt?" George added.

"We're about to find out," I said.

Linda gently removed my shoe. "Well, I see a nasty bruise already. Can you flex your foot forward?" she asked, supporting my ankle in her hand.

Wincing, I rotated my foot forward. "It hurts, but I can do it," I said.

"That a good sign," Linda said. "How about back?"

I flexed it back and gave her small nod.

"Good. Now tell me where it hurts," she said.

Carefully she worked her way up my foot, starting with my toes, softly applying pressure.

"There!" I yelped, instinctively yanking my foot out of her hand.

"Okay," Linda says. "I don't think it's broken. Probably very badly bruised. I'm going to get you some ice. You need to take it easy, use crutches for a few days, and take aspirin as needed for the pain." She headed toward the door to get the ice but stopped before leaving, turning back to face me. "You're a very lucky girl," she said. "This could have been much, much worse."

I let out a breath I hadn't even realized I was holding, so relieved that my foot wasn't broken.

"She's right," Bess said. "You are extremely lucky. If you hadn't gotten out of the way in time, that tree could have come down right on your head. Who knows what might have happened to you?"

"Yeah. I wish you could have seen yourself diving out of the way," George said. "You were like an action star. If I hadn't been so terrified, I would have recorded it. That dive was epic."

"That was pure luck," I said. "I wasn't even thinking! I just heard the cracking sound and my legs moved."

"Nancy, I'm so sorry," Maggie said. "If you hadn't been here helping me . . ."

I looked up at her. "This isn't your fault," I said. "I wanted to help you. There are risks involved in every case."

"You should go back to the hotel and rest," Bess said to Maggie.

Maggie looked torn. "I want to stay."

"You need to be ready for tonight. Bess and George are here. It'll be fine," I said.

Maggie hesitated. "I wouldn't feel right."

"Look, this isn't the first time I've been hurt on a case," I said, "and it won't be the last. Tonight is your big break. You need to do everything you can to be ready."

"If you're absolutely sure," Maggie said hesitantly.

"I'm positive," I said.

"Okay, Thank you again, Nancy, for everything you're doing," she said as she exited.

Bess, George, and I sat in silence for a moment.

"What's really lucky," I said, "is that the stage wasn't full. If Jamison hadn't wanted me to dance on my own, that stage would have been covered with people! Any one of them could have been injured."

"Do you think that was the plan?" George asked.

"I don't know," I said. "If several members of the corps de ballet were unable to dance tonight, that would ruin the show."

"And Maggie did get that note threatening her if she danced today," Bess said.

"Plus," George added, "she was onstage right before it fell. The suspect's timing could have been off."

"We need to take a look at that scenery and figure out why it fell."

There was a knock on the door.

"That must be Linda with the ice," Bess said, opening the door.

Only it wasn't Linda standing in the doorway. It was Jamison.

"We need to talk," Jamison said.

"Her foot is injured," George said.

"Yeah," Bess said. "She won't be able to dance tonight."

One look at the amused smirk on Jamison's face told me everything.

"He knows," I said to George and Bess.

"Did you really think I don't know who the members of my corps de ballet are?" Jamison asked.

"If you knew I wasn't part of your show, why did you make me dance? Why didn't you just kick me out?" I asked.

"You sneak into my rehearsal and you think I'm not at least going to have a little fun? I was going to let you humiliate yourself, and *then* kick you out, which I'm still going to do. Get out of my theater just as fast as you can hobble."

"You think Nancy's trying to ruin your show?" Bess asked.

"We've been on this tour for more than two weeks now. This is our tenth performance. Not one single thing has gone wrong in our nine previous shows, but we show up here, you three invade my theater, and suddenly the whole thing is falling apart. Explain that to me." He frowned and added curtly, "Or I'm calling the police."

"We're not causing the problems," I assured him. "We're trying to stop them. Someone is threatening Maggie. We're trying to figure out who before the show tonight."

Jamison laughed. "First of all, Maggie is being hazed. Every star dancer goes through it."

"No—" I started, but Jamison didn't stop to listen to what I had to stay.

"Second of all, a kid like you is a detective? Yeah, right." He headed to the door. "Get out of my theater and don't come back."

"I can't wait to see the look on his face when you *do* solve it," George said.

I tried to calm the anger bubbling inside of me, and instead slid myself forward on the table. "Hand me those crutches," I said to George. "We need to find out why that scenery fell—no matter what Jamison says."

It took longer than expected for me to wobble out to the stage on the crutches. By the time I got there, I was sweating and my arms were exhausted.

The theater was empty except for a few members of the stage crew, who were working fast to repair the scenery. Even still, the tree wasn't going to be perfect. There was no way they would be able to reattach a branch that had broken off.

I approached the crew member who looked like he was in charge. "Hi," I said.

I could see that he didn't want to waste time talking to me, but when he saw the crutches, his face softened.

"I'm really sorry about what happened to you, sweetheart. We're all just glad you're okay."

"Thanks," I said. "But I was wondering if you could tell me what went wrong. I thought the cables holding this tree were strong."

"They are," the guy said. He looked around to make sure no one was listening. "I shouldn't be telling you this—you seem like a sweet kid who caught a bad break—but this wasn't an accident."

"What do you mean?" I asked.

"Someone cut the wire."

I shook my head. "I was looking up right before the tree fell. There was no one there."

"Someone cut it a couple of days ago. Just enough so that it would fray little by little until it broke all the way."

My head shot up. "A couple of days ago?"

"Yeah," the guy said. "My bet is that it happened during load-in. That cable's been weakening for at least three days now."

Suddenly it all made sense. I had been right—we had been looking at it upside down this whole time. Bess and George saw my face and knew I had made a breakthrough.

"Thank you for your time," Bess said.

"You've been extremely helpful," George added as we made our way through the theater, my crutches clattering loudly.

"What is it, Nancy?" Bess asked.

"The cable was cut three days ago," I said.

"What's so important about that?" George asked.

"It was cut way before Maggie ever got the note at Hugo's."

"Right . . . ," Bess said.

"It didn't matter if Maggie hadn't come to rehearsal today. That scenery would have fallen no matter what."

"So . . . ," George said.

"The note wasn't a threat," I revealed. "It was a warning!"

I could see the gears turning in Bess's and George's minds as they put the pieces together.

"If that note was a warning . . . ," Bess said.

"Then Maggie's not the target," George completed for her.

"Exactly!" I said. "Someone is trying to ruin the entire show, not just Maggie's performance. Maggie's just a pawn."

CHAPTER ELEVEN

Recalculating

"IF THE CULPRIT ISN'T GOING AFTER MAGGIE, then who is the target?" Bess asked.

"Who else suffers if the show is a disaster in front of Oscar LeVigne?" I asked.

"Jamison?" George asked.

"Exactly," I said. "Sebastian said it last night. Maggie will have other shots—so will the rest of the dancers—but Jamison's getting older. If he doesn't break through soon, he'll never make it as a choreographer."

"It makes sense," George agreed. "Sebastian said

that if Maggie doesn't dance tonight, the show will be a catastrophe."

"So, who would want to sabotage Jamison?" I asked.

"Everyone in the company," George said, half-jokingly.

"It's true," Bess said. "We've seen him insult practically everyone and we've only been around for two days. Imagine listening to that every day on this tour."

"Or longer," George said. "He teaches at the academy, where a lot of these dancers are students. Some of them have heard him yelling for years."

"That leaves a lot of suspects, and the theater opens in two hours. What are we going to do?" asked Bess.

I looked at her. I knew what we had to do, but my friends weren't going to like it.

A few minutes later, I knocked on Jamison's office door.

"Are you sure this is a good idea?" George asked me for the third time in five minutes.

"It's all we can do," I said. "He's the only one who might have an idea who's behind this."

The door flew open. As soon as Jamison saw us, he rolled his eyes. "I thought I told you to get out."

"This is personal," I said. "Whoever is sabotaging Maggie wants you to fail. You're the real target for all of it."

Jamison shook his head. "Let's say I go along with your theory that what's been happening to Maggie is more than hazing. Why would anyone want me to fail?"

"Seriously?" George asked.

"You abuse people all day, telling them they're terrible at the thing they love the most, and it's never occurred to you that someone might want revenge?" Bess asked indignantly.

"You think what I do is abuse?" Jamison said, laughing.

"Yes," George said.

Jamison turned to me. "How did you feel when I questioned your abilities as a detective, when I talked down to you and needled you?"

"Angry," I admitted.

"And what else?"

I thought back to the fire I'd felt rise inside of me when he had called me a kid playing at detective. "I wanted to prove you wrong."

Jamison nodded. "I inspire greatness. Do you know what it takes to be great?" he asked.

"Practice," I said.

"Determination," George said.

"Discipline," Bess added.

"Yes, all of those," Jamison said. "And how do you keep pushing, keep going when you're tired? It's not by someone telling you you're doing well; it's by someone telling you that you can do better."

I understood what he was saying, and I knew that there was some truth to it. I had seen Maggie dance better after he had laid into her. I had even felt my own passion rise in the face of his dismissiveness, but I still wasn't convinced.

Bess wasn't either. "There have to be other ways to help besides telling them how awful they are."

Jamison shrugged. "I've turned out a lot of great dancers. When you've coached dozens of people to the apex of their abilities, we'll talk again about methodology."

"But what if someone with the potential to be the best can't take that kind of pressure and quits?" I asked.

A cloud passed over Jamison's face, but he quickly regained his composure. "Then that person could never truly be great, no matter what you thought, no matter how much you believed in them."

"Well, someone doesn't agree with your methods," I said, "and they're sabotaging your show. They started by harassing Maggie because they knew that without her the performance would flop. And when that didn't work, they tried to shut down the entire production by causing the scenery to fall. We don't know what else they're planning, but odds are it's something!"

"What do you want me to do?" Jamison asked. "Go around apologizing to everyone for making them feel bad?"

"It's probably too late for that," I said, "but it's not a bad idea. I think you should delay the show. Even if it's only by an hour, I would have a better shot of figuring out who did this."

"I can't do that. Oscar won't wait an hour for a show to start. If for some reason he did decide to wait, he'd be so prejudiced against the show it wouldn't matter how good it is; he'd still write it off as unprofessional."

I opened my mouth to protest, but Jamison kept talking.

"And I know Oscar. If he writes this show off, then he writes off Maggie as well. Do you want that? You know what a bad review will do to her career, right?"

"Yeah," I said. "Destroy it."

"Doors open in thirty minutes."

I was at a loss. I was tired. I was hungry. My foot hurt. I was out of leads and I was out of time.

Thirty minutes later Ned was waiting for us in the lobby with our tickets. He looked handsome wearing a tie under his sweater. My friends and I had gone back to Bess's house and changed into more appropriate clothing. I wore a simple black dress, while Bess had chosen a gorgeous purple gown with a beaded top. She was always the most fashionable of us. George, who hated dresses, was wearing a dark-green jumpsuit Bess had convinced her to wear. Under any other circumstances, we'd be taking pictures, but none of us felt like celebrating. While we had been changing I had hoped that I would have a flash of inspiration and suddenly know who the suspect was, but I was still flummoxed. I was convinced something horrible would happen during the show and all I would be able to do was watch. Instead of looking forward to the performance, I was dreading it.

"Nancy! Are you okay?" Ned said, rushing over to me.

I quickly told him about the tree falling, and George reenacted my dive out of the way.

"I'm fine," I said. "It's just bruised. I'll be walking on two feet again in a few days."

"Well, please tell me you at least caught the person responsible."

I shook my head.

Ned kissed the top of my head gently. "Well,

there's still time," he said. "I believe you can do this."

All the determination that had wilted out of me earlier came roaring back. I wished Jamison had been there to see this. There were other ways to inspire people to do their best aside from yelling and screaming.

I looked up at Ned. "Thank you," I said sincerely.

"Of course," he said. "Anyway, I don't know anything about this case, except what you told me last night on the phone, but I'm ready to do whatever you need. What's our next step?"

I bit my thumb as I thought. "When we were investigating, we focused entirely on Maggie," I said. "We need to rethink everything, concentrating on Jamison. Are there any assumptions we're making?"

George tapped her foot as she thought, while Bess looked at the ceiling. My eyes wandered as I let my mind drift over everything that had happened. A short, balding man dressed in a three-piece suit strode into the theater. I knew instantly that this was Oscar LeVigne. Miss Taylor quickly came up to him and introduced herself.

Oscar gave her a once-over and then turned away. Miss Taylor hurried after him.

"Maggie Rogers, the star of the performance, got her start right here in River Heights. At my school," she said. "You know how important the early training is. All the habits are established in the first four years."

"Excuse me," Oscar said. "I need to find the men's room." He walked away, leaving Miss Taylor blushing in embarrassment.

"We assumed the culprit was Maggie's peer," I said. "That it was another dancer."

"Yeah . . . ," George said.

"But if this is about Jamison, wouldn't it make more sense that it would be one of his peers?"

"You're not saying what I think you're saying, are you, Nancy?" Bess asked. "You know Miss Taylor couldn't do something like this."

"I know it seems like a long shot, but think about it, Bess," I said. "She's around the theater all the time. She can go anywhere she likes. She had access to the poster files."

"But Maggie's her star student. Maggie doing well tonight will only help her. Why would she jeopardize that?" Bess asked.

"Jealousy makes people do crazy things," I said. "I doubt her dreams included teaching in a small town. She probably had bigger ambitions in her life too. Maybe she really wanted to be a choreographer. Sebastian said that all the teachers in the area applied to lead this tour. Maybe Miss Taylor applied, and she's mad that Jamison was selected instead of her."

"You don't have proof," Bess insisted. "You have no idea if Miss Taylor applied to choreograph this show."

"We need to find out," George said. "We have only a few minutes to pursue this lead."

George was right. I made my way over to Miss Taylor. Ordinarily, I would carefully craft the tactic I was going to take, but I didn't have time to come up with an elaborate ruse this time. I was just going to have to wing it.

"After seeing Jamison with his dancers, I'm so glad

you were my ballet teacher, instead of him," I said as I approached her.

"That man is a monster," Miss Taylor hissed. She quickly covered her mouth. "Forgive me. I shouldn't say that. It just drives me crazy that he's being rewarded, even though he tortures his students. Some of us nurture our students. We should be the ones showing off what we can do to Oscar LeVigne, not the man who caused one of his students to suffer a nervous breakdown within two months of joining the New York City Ballet."

My head shot up. Jamison and the New York City Ballet . . . I knew I had heard something about that earlier, but I couldn't place it. Between the length of the day and the pain in my foot, my brain felt sluggish. I needed my friends to help me puzzle it out.

Around us the lights in the lobby started flashing.

"We'd better take our seats," she said with a smile.

"I'll be there in a minute," I said.

"Make it quick. You don't want to miss it." She headed inside the theater. A few feet away, she stopped and turned back. "Nancy, please don't say anything about what I told you. I know the parents of the ballerina I mentioned are very protective of her privacy. They've worked really hard not to let it get out beyond a small group of people. I just happen to have a friend at the New York City Ballet who told me."

I nodded as I hobbled back to my friends.

"What'd you find out?" Bess asked.

The ushers were giving us dirty looks. We had three minutes until curtain time.

"Well, she's definitely bitter," I said. I hesitated for a second. I knew Miss Taylor had asked me not to tell, but this was a big clue and I needed their help. "This is a secret, but she said Jamison causes his students to have nervous breakdowns, including one who made it into the New York City Ballet," I said.

"Didn't Maggie say that Jamison only had one student who made it into that company?" Bess asked.

All of a sudden it came back to me "Yes! Veronica, Sebastian's sister!" I said.

My brain raced, no longer sluggish, as the pieces

snapped into place. Sebastian had easy access to Maggie's phone. He handled odd jobs for Jamison all the time. He easily could have altered the poster. He was also at the restaurant with us, giving him plenty of opportunity to leave the note.

"It's Sebastian!" I announced. "He's getting revenge on his sister's behalf."

Inside, the house lights went down. The ushers shut the theater doors as the piano started playing.

George, Bess, and I all stared at one another in horror.

CHAPTER TWELVE

~

Showtime

"WHAT DO WE DO?" BESS ASKED.

"You know he has something planned," George said. "This guy was a professional piano player by age fourteen. He's determined."

"We need to get into his dressing room," I said. "Maybe there's a clue in there."

"How do we get there?" Ned asked.

"Around back," Bess said. "There's a stage door we can go through."

"We have to go outside and around the building?" Ned asked.

Bess nodded. Ned looked at me on my crutches. After a beat, he wrapped his arm around me, handed my crutches to George, and swooped me up, holding me like a baby.

"Forgive the indignity," Ned said, "but this is going to be a lot faster than you hobbling through the snow. Safer, too."

"All right," I said, "Let's find out what Sebastian is up to."

As we made our way around the building to the stage door, I was glad that it was cold and the area outside the theater was empty. We must have made for an odd sight: the four of us sneaking through the parking lot, George and Bess each carrying a crutch, and Ned carrying me.

Bess opened the stage door and Ned put me down. I got my crutches back and we made our way down the hall.

We made it past the greenroom, where all the dancers who weren't onstage waited their turn. A group of them played cards. Others were on their cell phones.

A few stretched. A video feed showed the performance onstage, so they could see when they needed to get to the wings.

"This is it," Bess said, pointing to a door on the right. She tried the knob, but it was locked.

"Now what?" George asked.

"I can probably break in," Ned said, leaning back to throw his shoulder against the door.

"I have a better idea," I said, nodding at George. She grinned, reached into her bag, and pulled out a set of lock picks. "No need for both of us to get hurt."

"I wouldn't have been hurt," Ned protested.

"Did you get a new set?" I asked George as she knelt in front of the lock.

"My aunt gave me some money for Christmas," George explained. "It was either this or a GPS tracker." She stuck two picks in the lock and started working one around inside carefully, sticking her tongue out unconsciously as she tried to manipulate the pin inside the lock. George had taught me some of the rudimentary principles of lock picking, but it was as much an art form as a science, and George had the magic touch.

Sweat beaded on her forehead as she continued to work. Her brow creased in worry. I could feel myself starting to get anxious that this was taking too long, but I didn't say anything. I didn't want George to feel any more pressure.

"I could still break it open," Ned said.

"Got it!" George exclaimed. She turned the knob and we were in.

We scanned the room, which was incredibly tidy. Sebastian's casual clothes hung neatly in a closet. Piles of sheet music sat on a table. There was a backpack in the corner.

"Are you sure there's going to be a clue in here?" Ned asked. "This room looks barren."

"There has to be something. The app on Maggie's phone, the poster, the scenery—all required research and planning. Sebastian hasn't done anything spontaneous. If my hunch is right, he's been thinking about getting revenge on Jamison for a long time.

We'll find something that indicates what he has planned next."

We stepped farther into the room. Bess took the desk, George went to the vanity, Ned sprinted to the closet, and I headed toward the backpack in the corner.

"If there's anything that seems weird, flag it. It could be a clue. Sebastian is smart. It may not be obvious what his plan is."

I could hear my friends opening drawers and rummaging through Sebastian's belongings as I dumped the contents of the bag onto the floor. A phone charger, some gum, a toiletries kit, and an old photo album. I flipped through the photos. They were all of him and his sister. It started when they were preschool age and ended with Veronica holding up her offer letter from the New York City Ballet. From the pictures, it was clear that they were incredibly close. They were always hugging and smiling and genuinely seemed to be proud of each other and all their accomplishments. Even though I knew that what

Sebastian was doing was wrong, I could understand the pain he felt seeing his sister suffer.

But I didn't see a single clue. Just for the sake of doing something, I emptied the toiletries kit on the table, but all it had was a toothbrush, deodorant, a comb, and a bottle of talcum powder.

George came over. "Nothing of note in the closet. You find anything?"

I shook my head.

"The only thing I've learned is that this guy must have really stinky feet."

"What do you mean?" I asked.

"How much talcum powder does one guy need?" George asked, picking up the bottle that was on the table.

"You found talcum powder too?" I asked.

"Yeah, a bottle about three-quarters full." She shook the bottle. "This one has less, but it's still at least half full."

"Can I see the bottle you found on the vanity?" I asked George.

George brought it back to me. The bottle was the

same size and color as the talcum powder I'd found, but the logo was different. I looked closer.

"This isn't talcum powder. This is orthochloro-benzalmalononitrile," I said, sounding it out.

"In English?" George asked.

"That's the main chemical in tear gas!" Ned exclaimed. "We talked about it in my chemistry class last semester. Tear gas is actually a powder."

I hastily set the bottle down.

"It has to get over a certain temperature to emit a gas, which is when it causes all the symptoms, like crying, sneezing, difficulty breathing, and so on," Ned continued.

"Is there a way Sebastian could get the stage area hot enough to emit the gas?" I asked. "Having a bunch of dancers onstage crying and coughing is going to make the choreography look pretty bad."

"The Fresnels," George said. "They're the biggest lights, and they get really hot. I heard the crew talking about it when I was undercover. If you touch them without gloves, you can actually burn your flesh."

"That's disgusting," Bess said.

"We have to get those lights turned off," I said.

Ned scooped me up again, George and Bess grabbed my crutches, and we made it back to the front door of the theater.

Ignoring the ushers who tried to stop us, we entered the theater as quietly as we could. A few people turned to glare at us, and I felt bad for distracting them, but I reminded myself that getting hit by tear gas would be even more distracting. George led the way to the lighting booth, and we pushed our way in, shutting the door behind us.

Jamison sat in the booth behind the crew member running the board, watching the show. His head snapped toward us. It was tight quarters with all of us piled in.

"Are you kidding me? How many times and how many different ways do I have to tell you to get out of my theater?"

The crew member working the lighting board stayed focused on the show, studiously ignoring the commotion we were causing.

"You have to turn off the Fresnels," I said.

Jamison turned to the board operator. "Don't you dare turn those lights off, Kevin." He turned back to us. "Forget the police. I'm having you sent straight to the loony bin, because you have clearly lost your mind. If we cut the Fresnels, three-quarters of the stage will be dark."

"Better than one hundred percent of the dancers crying and coughing," George said.

"What on earth are you prattling on about? None of you are making any sense."

"Sebastian put tear gas on the Fresnels. When the lights get hot enough, tear gas will spread through this entire theater," I said.

Jamison opened his mouth, presumably to tell us we were crazy again, but he paused. I could see him putting the pieces together.

"Do you have definitive proof?" he asked.

"We found this in Sebastian's dressing room," Bess said, handing Jamison the bottle of tear gas.

"I don't buy it," Jamison said.

"That's proof," George said, exasperated. "What more do you want?"

"I don't know what orthochlorobenzalmalononitrile even is," he scoffed. "You could be pulling a prank on me, getting me back for belittling you earlier."

"If you didn't treat people so badly, you wouldn't have to worry about that," Bess muttered under her breath.

Onstage, a dancer sneezed. "It's starting," I said to Kevin, the board operator. If Jamison wouldn't see sense, maybe I could appeal to Kevin. "You have to turn off the lights right now."

Kevin looked at Jamison, clearly unsure what to do. "Don't do it," Jamison ordered.

From the stage, another sneeze. "Kevin, come on," I implored.

Now a cough. If we didn't cut those lights now, it was only going to get worse.

Kevin looked back and forth between me and Jamison. I could see the gears turning in his head as he tried to figure out who he should listen to.

Another cough.

"Kevin—" Jamison started, but before could finish, Kevin sprang into action.

"I'm sorry. Don't kill me," Kevin said as his hands flew over the lighting board, and suddenly, just as Jamison had predicted, more than half the stage was dark. The audience gasped, but Jamison had trained his dancers well. They kept going as if nothing had happened.

"Thank you," I said to Kevin. "You did the right thing. Now can you make sure that a crew member removes the powder from the lights at intermission?"

He nodded.

For the first time since we'd encountered him, Jamison was speechless. He seemed completely in shock. I wasn't going to wait around for him to start yelling again. I turned back to my friends. "Let's get backstage and tell Maggie the case is solved," I said. "Her big solo is right after intermission. I want her to feel completely confident."

Backstage was chaos. Intermission had just started, and the dancers were all abuzz about the lights going out. We couldn't find Maggie anywhere.

"Where's Maggie?" I asked Fiona.

"I think I saw her go into Sebastian's dressing room," Fiona said.

We rushed there as fast as we could.

The door was locked, but we could hear the muffled sound of Maggie crying. "Why are you doing this? I thought you were my friend!"

"My turn," Ned said, as he put his shoulder into the door with all his might. The door flew open with a groan. Maggie was tied to the chair and Sebastian was pacing in front of her.

"I'm sorry," he was saying. "I was trying to protect you. But Jamison cut the lights. He knows about the tear gas. There's no other way to destroy Jamison and save you from him."

"Sebastian," I said. "I know why you're doing it, but this isn't justice. This isn't taking care of Maggie."

He looked over at me, completely destroyed.

"I told her not to dance tonight. I didn't want Maggie to get hurt, but Jamison broke her. He needs to pay," Sebastian said.

"Not like this," I said. "Innocent people could have been really hurt from the tree falling. And the tear gas!"

"What are you talking about? Who needs to pay?" Maggie asked from the chair.

"You have to tell her," I said to Sebastian.

He looked at me, then glanced at Ned, George, and Bess blocking the exit.

"Jamison. He needs to pay . . . for what he did to Veronica."

Maggie looked at him confused. "He got her into the New York City Ballet," she began.

Sebastian looked enraged. "But at what cost? He got her into the New York City Ballet, but now she's in a mental institution. You want to know why she doesn't return your calls? It's because she's not allowed access to her phone."

"What?" Maggie said, shocked.

"Veronica loved to dance . . . until she met Jamison. Then nothing she did was ever good enough. He kept pushing her, critiquing every little thing she did. He insulted her. Told her she didn't work hard enough, but all she ever did was work. You saw her."

"But that's how you become great," Maggie said.

Sebastian shook his head. "You didn't see her in the months before she left. You were in Paris on that exchange program, but she was a nervous wreck. When she finally got to New York, she said she could still hear Jamison's voice echoing through her head, all day, every day. With the added competition and the pressure, she lost it. Next thing we knew, we were getting a call from the emergency room that Veronica had been admitted due to a nervous breakdown." He paused and knelt in front of Maggie. "I saw him doing the same thing to you, and I couldn't stand it. I couldn't let him destroy you like he destroyed Veronica."

Tears ran down Maggie's face. "I can take it," she said. "I promise. He's not going to destroy me."

"Ruining Maggie's shot," I told him, "will destroy Maggie—just like Jamison pushing Veronica broke her. It would make you no better than him." Out of the corner of my eye, I spotted Ned moving toward Sebastian. I had to keep Sebastian focused on me and away from Ned. "I know you don't want to do that," I said, saying anything that came into my mind, just to keep him interested. "You care about Maggie. She's like another sister to you."

Suddenly Ned pounced, tackling Sebastian and restraining him. Bess rushed over to untie Maggie. Sebastian didn't struggle. It was like Ned had literally knocked all the fight out of him. Instead he collapsed into a heap, heaving loud sobs. Maggie stared, as if she didn't know who he was.

In the hallway, dancers yelled that there was only one more minute of intermission.

"Time for your solo," I said to Maggie.

Maggie hesitated, still trying to process everything that had happened.

"Go," I said. "Show Oscar what you're made of." Maggie looked at me, still mystified, but then her face morphed, and I saw the serious dancer. I knew she wouldn't let anything get in her way.

"Thank you," she said. She walked toward the stage with a determined gait.

After Maggie had hurried out, I turned to my friends. "Ned and I will stay here with Sebastian, just to make sure he doesn't try anything else, and then we'll call the police as soon as the performance is over. I don't want them bursting in and ending the show. You guys go tell Jamison that he's going to need to play the piano during the second half."

After George and Bess hurried off, I convinced Sebastian and Ned to move to the greenroom. The other dancers gave us space. Information spreads quickly among tight-knit groups; I could tell they already knew everything. Sebastian curled up on the couch. I looked at his thin body, which looked small and broken. I knew I should feel victorious—this had been a hard case—but instead I felt sad. This wasn't how I had wanted it to end.

Ned and I watched Maggie dance her solo on the greenroom's TV. The video feed was silent, so we couldn't hear the music, but we could tell that she had nailed it.

As soon as the last dancer had taken her curtsy,

I called the police. Ten minutes later, two officers escorted Sebastian out of the building. As Ned and I stood in front of the theater and watched them take him away, I fought back tears.

"Obviously, Sebastian went way too far," I said. "But I understand why he thought he needed to do it."

"He was in a tough spot," Ned agreed. "I feel for him and his sister."

"Jamison destroyed both of them," I said.

"It's freezing," Ned said. "Let's get back inside and find the others."

As we turned around to go back inside, we noticed Jamison standing behind me, watching the patrol car drive away. There was a pensive look on his face, but when I tried to catch his eye, he avoided looking at me.

We found George and Bess in the lobby. A little later Maggie came out.

"Sorry I took so long," Maggie said. "Jamison pulled us all aside afterward and gave us a speech about how he knows he doesn't tell us enough that we're doing well. He wanted us to know that he was proud of us."

"Wow," I said.

"Yeah," Maggie agreed. "Weird coming from him, but nice." She paused for a moment. "What's going to happen to Sebastian?"

"I don't know," I said. "Hopefully he'll get some help."

"Yeah," Maggie said softly.

"Excuse me," a deep male voice interrupted us.

We turned to see Oscar LeVigne. He held out his hand toward Maggie, ignoring the rest of us. "I just wanted to say that I'm so glad I was able to witness such a breakthrough performance. You are a rising talent!"

"Thank you," Maggie said, shaking his hand. "I really appreciate you coming out here to see our show."

Oscar nodded and walked away. As soon as he was out the door, Maggie turned back to us with a huge smile on her face.

After we calmed down, we decided to go out for dessert to celebrate. Maggie even admitted that she had earned it.

We stepped into the cold air and spotted Mike standing on the theater steps with Colin.

"Oh no," George said. "Not again."

But as we got closer, we saw that Mike wasn't yelling. He stretched his arm out and awkwardly placed his hand on Colin's shoulder. "You were good up there," Mike said stiffly.

Colin looked at him, shocked, and then broke into a big grin. "You watched?"

"You have a very persuasive young lady for a friend," Mike explained.

We walked past Mike's car and saw Fiona sitting inside, watching Mike and Colin nervously. She couldn't hear them from her vantage point. As we walked past, I shot her a thumbs-up sign. A huge look of relief passed over her face.

Since I couldn't drive, we piled into Ned's car.

"I have an announcement," Bess said. We all turned to look at her. "I signed up for tap-dancing classes."

"What?" George asked.

"I feel like I've quit too many things because I was worried that I wasn't the best or it wouldn't lead anywhere, but I realized these past couple of days that it's okay to do something just because you like it. Of all the classes and lessons I took when I was younger, tap was my favorite."

"That's great," Ned said.

"So, is tap dancing your thing?" I asked Bess.

"Maybe," she said with a smile. "But if it's not, I'll try something else."

I squeezed her hand, happy for her.

We sat in silence. I looked around the car and felt a warmth spread over me despite the freezing temperatures outside. As much as I loved solving a case, nothing made me happier than being surrounded by my friends. I hoped I never forgot that, no matter how great a detective I became.

Dear Diary,

MAGGIE GOT AN OFFER FROM THE CHICAGO Ballet Company a few days later. She was ecstatic! I guess Jamison's teaching methods got results. Even so, I hoped Sebastian ended up okay. He had good reasons for confronting Jamison, but he went about it all wrong. The good thing is that Jamison seemed to learn a lesson; he started giving his students positive reinforcement. Even if someone can do better, you should still remind them when they do well.

READ WHAT HAPPENS IN THE NEXT MYSTERY

IN THE NANCY DREW DIARIES,

The Sign in the Smoke

Dear Diary,

NO ONE LOVES WARM WEATHER MORE than me! But since trouble seems to find me even when the sun's glaring down, my summers usually aren't so relaxing. I decided that this year, however, all that would change. I was going to take a much-needed _self-imposed_ summer break from sleuthing!

So when Bess suggested that she, George, and I sign up as counselors at Camp Cedarbark, I thought it was a great idea. I figured I'd spend time with the kids, make a few new friends, maybe even pick up a hobby. Of course, I should have known that escaping mystery-fueled drama is never as easy as it seems. . . .

A Summer Retirement

BESS PEERED DOWN INTO HER CUP AND then thrust it back at the girl who'd handed it to her. "Could I get just a *smidge* more marshmallow?"

"*More* marshmallow?" her cousin George asked, swirling her plastic spoon through her own pile of Strawberry Cheesecake Explosion. "If you get any more marshmallow, Bess, all of your organs are going to stick together."

My boyfriend, Ned, cleared his throat. "I'm pretty sure that's not how the human digestive system works," he said, watching as the ice cream scooper handed the cup back to Bess, "but you *are* going to have the mother of sugar highs."

Bess tilted her head at him. "After eating an ice cream sundae? You don't say." She smiled at the ice cream scooper, plunged her spoon into a fluffy cloud of marshmallow, and shoveled it into her mouth, closing her eyes in pleasure. "Ohhhh, yeah. That's the stuff. Besides"—she opened her eyes—"we're celebrating here. At least, Nancy, George and I are. Aren't we?"

"We sure are," I agreed, stepping up to the counter. "Can I get a strawberry sundae with Oreo chip and whipped cream?"

Ned smiled at me. "Good combination."

"Thanks," I said. "I spent all winter planning the ultimate sundae combo."

Bess took another bite of her sundae and moaned. "And we can spend *all day* eating ice cream now, guys," she said happily. "Because as of midnight last night, it's officially *summer!*"

"For twelve beautiful, short weeks," Ned put in.

Bess glared at him. "Buzzkill."

"And then comes fall," Ned said, taking a lick of his own rocky-road-with-sprinkles cone. "Then winter. It'll be snowing before we know it!"

"My *point* is," Bess said, raising her spoon in the air, "that we girls have three months of gorgeous weather stretching ahead of us. *Three months.* What are we going to do with it all?"

I took my sundae from the ice cream scooper and handed over my money. "Um, if I were to guess? I'll probably end up solving a mystery or something."

"You're so predictable, Nance," George scoffed, rolling her eyes.

I took a bite of my sundae. *Ooh*, it was perfect. I'd done it. I'd created the ultimate sundae. "I dunno," I said, shrugging at George. "Maybe I'll take the summer off from solving mysteries. Take up knitting or something."

Now it was Bess's turn to roll her eyes.

"What?" I asked.

"I'll believe that when I see it, is all," she explained. "How are you going to manage it? Mysteries tend to find you, you know. I think the only way you could pull that off is to stop talking to people at all."

George nodded, chewing on a nugget of cheesecake. "Or go on a really long trip," she added.

"Where you don't speak the language," Ned put in, pausing from licking his cone.

"You *guys!*" I said, getting frustrated. "I'm serious. I mean, kind of."

"You want to stop solving mysteries?" Bess asked, looking incredulous. She slapped a hand over my forehead. "Are you feeling okay?"

I dodged out from under her. "Not *permanently,*" I said. "But it might be nice to just relax this summer. Enjoy nature. Maybe play some sports."

I expected Bess to laugh again, but instead she looked thoughtful. "I think George might be right," she said slowly. "I think to do that, you might have to leave town. And I have an idea!" She put her sundae down on a nearby table and then swung her purse off her shoulder so she could start digging in it. Normally this was a twenty-minute process, minimum, so George and I looked at each other and sat down to continue eating our ice cream. But just as I had the perfect mouthful of strawberries, ice cream, and whipped cream, Bess pulled out a glossy brochure and waved it at me.

"Um," I said, struggling to swallow what I had in my mouth, "okay."

I took the brochure. The cover showed a beautiful lake surrounded by woods and cabins, and blocky text spelled out CAMP CEDARBARK.

I raised an eyebrow at Bess. "I think we're a little old for summer camp, don't you think?"

Bess, who'd sat down with us and was inhaling her sundae, sighed. "Not as *campers*," she said. "As *counselors*. Think about it, Nance. You want to relax, enjoy nature, maybe play some sports?"

"Yeah." George snorted. "There's nothing more relaxing than looking after six children who belong to someone else all summer long!"

Bess frowned at her. "Shush. You like kids." She turned back to me. "And it wouldn't be for the whole summer. Camp Cedarbark does little mini-sessions, each one week long! Besides, it's not just any camp, Nancy. I used to go there when I was a kid!"

I squinted at the brochure. "I thought you went to Camp Lark-something?"

"Camp Larksong," Bess confirmed. "But they closed five years ago, two years after my last visit! Now a Camp Larksong alum has finally bought the place and restored it. They sent this brochure to all the former Camp Larksong campers, encouraging us to get involved or send our kids."

"Kids?" asked Ned.

Bess shrugged. "Well, Camp Larksong was in business for twenty-three years, so . . ." She turned to me, her face as eager as a puppy's. "What do you think?"

I raised my eyebrows. "You're serious?"

"Why wouldn't I be?" Bess stuck out her lower lip in a pout. "I have so many happy memories of this place! I was sort of thinking of applying to be a counselor on my own, but it would be so much more fun with you guys!"

George looked at her cousin. "You really think I could take care of a bunkful of children and not lose my mind?"

"You'd have *help*," Bess admonished her. "We'd each be assigned a CIT, counselor-in-training, who's a few years younger. And of course, we'd all be there to help each other. Besides"—she pointed an accusing finger at George—"you *like* children. You're a great babysitter! Remember when you watched cousin Gemma for the day and taught her how to code?"

George's lips turned up. "Well, *she* was an exceptional kid. She had a natural talent!"

"I guess we'd have activities to keep them busy, George," I said, trying to imagine the three of us relaxing by the lake in the photo. "It's not like we'd be starting from scratch."

"And the activities are *really fun*," Bess went on. "I know neither of you went to summer camp, but it's the greatest! Swimming and hiking and playing capture the flag and . . ."

I looked at George. Bess was right, I'd never been

to summer camp . . . but it *did* sound really fun. And definitely more exciting than sitting in our backyard rereading Harry Potter with my feet in a kiddie pool, which was basically last summer. (When I wasn't sleuthing, that is.) "It would only be a week or two," I said quietly.

Bess looked at me, her eyes bulging in excitement as she realized she'd gained an ally. "Ten days," she squealed. "The mini-sessions are just one week of camp, and three days' training. That's not so bad, right? Even if you hated it, it's *only* ten days."

The silence that followed was broken by a *crunch!* We all turned to see Ned finishing up his waffle cone. "I'm sold," he said after he swallowed. "But unfortunately, I'm using the summer to bang out my science requirements. You're on your own, Nance."

Bess smiled at him. "You weren't invited anyway," she said. "It's a girls' camp. What do you say?" she asked, looking eagerly from me to George.

"I'm . . . *in*," I said, smiling in spite of myself. A week at camp! It was the last way I thought I'd spend my summer, and yet it was somehow perfect. I looked back down at the photo on the brochure. It looked . . . *peaceful.*

Bess squealed and turned to George, squeezing her arm. "It's on you, cuz," she said, looking George in the eye. "You *know* this would be fun. Come on. Everything I suggest for us turns out to be fun!"

I held up my hand. *"Actually . . ."*

Ned raised a finger in the air. "Yeah, I'm gonna have to object to that one too."

George laughed.

Bess pretended to glare at me. "We're still all *alive,* anyway," she pointed out. Then she turned back to George. "Cuz, will you make my summer? Come on, say you're in."

George took the brochure from me and looked down at the photo. A slow smile crept across her face. "Okay," she said. "But if I get a bunkful of princessy mean girls, I am *coming for you in the night,* Bess."

"I can live with that," she said quickly. "I'm fast. I know how to hide. Anyway, *yay!*" She grabbed me suddenly around the waist with one hand, pulling in George with the other. "Group hug! We're headed back to Camp Larksong!"

Six weeks and endless application forms later, I sat on my bed, cramming in my last two T-shirts into my camp duffel bag. Our housekeeper, Hannah, had helped me sew labels bearing my name onto all my clothes. Eight shirts, six pairs of shorts, two pairs of jeans, pj's, one casual dress—I was officially ready to go!

And not a minute too soon, because as soon as I zipped up my bag, I heard the toot of Bess's horn in the driveway. I hefted my bag onto my shoulder—*whoa, I hope I don't have to carry this far*—and maneuvered it down the stairs and into the front hall. Dad and Hannah, having heard the horn too, were standing there waiting to say good-bye.

Dad grinned at me. "I can't believe you're going to *camp*," he said, shaking his head. "You were never a *camp* type. You were a stick-your-nose-in-a-book type."

"It looks really fun, Dad," I said. "Besides, it's a

great excuse to spend some time outside and get to know some new people."

He nodded. "I know you'll have fun," he said, and leaned in for a hug.

"Don't forget to eat," Hannah advised as I finished up Dad's hug and went to hug her. "You'll be running around a lot!"

I chuckled. "Well, I can guarantee the food won't be as good as yours," I promised. "I'll miss you both. Write to me?"

Dad pulled out some folded paper and a pre-addressed envelope from his shirt pocket. "Ready to go," he promised. "Don't worry, you won't miss any of the big news from River Heights."

"I love you both," I said, opening the door and squeezing through with my bag.

"Love you, too. Have fun," Dad said, leaning out to take the door from me and waving in Bess's direction. "Don't get in too much trouble."

I grinned back at him. "When have *I* ever gotten in trouble?"

I hauled my bag out to Bess's coupe and loaded it into the trunk, then climbed into the passenger seat. Bess was all smiley and pumped up, and couldn't stop talking about all the fun we were going to have at Camp Cedarbark. She explained that at Camp Larksong, each week ended with a special campout on a hill by the lake, with a sunset sing-along and ghost stories around the campfire. She'd read on Camp Cedarbark's website that they were planning to continue the tradition.

We swung by George's house, where she was waiting in the driveway with her parents. After lots of hugs and kisses (George is an only child, and her parents *love* her), George climbed into the backseat and we were off.

"Aren't you *excited*?" Bess asked, peering at her cousin in the rearview mirror when we were stopped at a traffic light. "Aren't we going to have the *best time ever*?"

"Yeeeeeeah," said George slowly. But she didn't look like she thought we were going to have the *best time ever*. She looked a little . . . concerned.

"Is something up?" I asked.

"Not exactly," she said. But she still wore a confused expression. "It's just . . . I Googled 'Camp Larksong' and 'Camp Cedarbark' last night."

The light changed, and Bess punched the gas with a little too much force. We lurched forward. "Don't tell me you found some nasty review," she said. "I've been looking at them every few weeks myself. Everyone says they've had an amazing time there."

"It wasn't a nasty review," George said, shaking her head. "It was a newspaper article. The headline was 'Tragedy Closes Camp Larksong.' It was dated five years ago—the year you said the camp closed."

Bess frowned. "That's strange. I never heard about any tragedy. What did the article say?"

George hesitated. "That's just the thing—I couldn't access the article. It was taken down a year ago. I just found a link to the cached page."

Bess looked thoughtful as she pulled onto the highway. For a moment, we were all silent as she merged into traffic and we all thought our separate thoughts.

"I'm sure it's nothing," Bess said after a minute or two, startling me. "If there were really some big tragedy, I would have heard about it, right? I kept in touch with some of my fellow campers for years. Nobody mentioned anything."

"I guess," George said, but she was staring out the window with a pensive expression.

Things got quiet again for a while, and I tried to lose myself in the landscape whooshing by and ignore the little worried voice inside my head.

The voice that said, *Please don't let there be a mystery to solve at Camp Cedarbark!*

IF YOU ♥ THIS BOOK,
you'll love all the rest from

YOUR HOME AWAY FROM HOME:

AladdinMix.com

HERE YOU'LL GET:

- ♥ The first look at new releases
- ♥ Chapter excerpts from all the Aladdin M!X books
- ♥ Videos of your fave authors being interviewed

FOR ACTIVITIES, STICKERS, AND MORE, JOIN THE ACADEMY AT GODDESSGIRLSBOOKS.COM!